REAP THE NIGHT
A FORBIDDEN REAPER ROMANCE

L.E. PEREZ

Copyright 2019 by L.E. Perez, Palmas Publishing

All rights reserved. Published in the United States by Palmas Publishing

This book is a work of fiction. Any references to historical events, real people, or real locales are used fictitiously. Other names, characters, places, and incidents are the product of the author's imagination and/or are provided for use in the Hotel Paranormal Series, and any resemblance to actual events or locales or persons, living or dead, is entirely coincidental.

No part of this publication may be reproduced, stored in a retrieval system or transmitted in any form or by any means, electronic, mechanical, photocopying, recording, or otherwise, without written permission of the publisher.

For information regarding permission, email:
Palmas Publishing
PalmasPublishing@Gmail.com

For my love, my inspiration, Maria

PROLOGUE

It was a good night for Reapers. The body count on the highway was high thanks to the explosion smack in the middle of the pileup by one of the tankers.

It should have been easy to take those lives, but the accident caused a frenzy of sorts and even those expected to survive, died. Caught in the middle of dire and unexplainable circumstances, people panicked.

The Reapers on that night were there on explicit orders and they followed them to the letter, until one didn't.

CHAPTER ONE

Alex Dante pushed through the double doors and shook herself off, trying to get the dust and grime off her long leather duster. Tossing her canvas duffel down, she kicked her boots against the doorframe to get some of the caked-on mud off. She always felt a bit dirty after a job but this one had been dirtier then most.

Being a Reaper sucked sometimes, but it was her lot in life and it kept her whole.

The opulence of the lobby she walked into always took her by surprise. It wasn't that she was unfamiliar with luxury, rather it was the stark contrast with the ugliness she faced in her job on a daily basis that bore absolutely no resemblance to this.

The Hotel Paranormal was one of her go to places. Lately, more of a home than any one place she'd ever stayed besides the Academie and when things were rocky, this was her refuge.

She took a deep calming breath and grabbed her duffel before swaggering over to the front desk to check in.

"Hey beautiful." Alex smiled knowing her husky voice sent Ava all atwitter.

Ava was a shy, mousy little thing, pretty in her own way. Alex always made a point of talking to her even though most of the Hotel's guests acted like Ava didn't exist. Everyone mattered to Alex. That would be a joke if it wasn't so sad. She didn't have many friends in her line of work and if she could get one smile from someone, it made her day.

Today was her day.

When Ava looked up, she gave Alex her best smile.

"Your room is ready Ms. Dante."

"Alex, Ava. I told you, please call me Alex."

Head down Ava tried to smother her giggle with her hand. "Yes Ms. Alex, your room is ready."

"Thanks darling." She moved to swing the duffle up to her shoulder and found she couldn't.

David, the hotel's miniature bellhop had hold of one strap.

"Allow me Ms. Alex." Small as he was, he hefted the duffle over one shoulder with ease.

She gave him a crooked smile for using her first name. He must have overheard her.

"Thank you, David. My usual room I believe, right Ava?"

"Yes ma'am."

"Good. I'll leave you to it then. I need a drink." An air of melancholy washed over her as the reality of her stay hit her again.

For now, this was her safe place. Where she sometimes went to regroup and right now, she needed to re-evaluate everything there was about being a Reaper. She turned on her heel without another word and headed toward the bar.

Alex barely acknowledged the greetings from the beings who recognized her as she walked through the lobby. She had one focus right now. A drink.

The moment she took a seat at the counter, a beautifully manicured hand placed a shot of the bar's best tequila in front of her.

Alex growled as she grabbed it and downed it without a word.

Again, the hand placed a shot down in front of her but this time it covered her drink.

"Bad day love?"

Normally the soft lilt would bring a smile to her face, but not this time. Alex gently but firmly took Selena's hand off the shot glass and threw that one back as well.

She tried to force a smile. "You could say that."

"Hmm." Selena poured another glass. "Would you like to talk about it?"

"Not right now, maybe another time. Do you mind just leaving the bottle with me?"

Selena hesitated.

Alex Dante never indulged this way, and everyone knew it. There were a lot of beings who frequented the Hotel. In their own ways, they were all creatures of habit, but Alex never quite fit the mold and Selena like everyone else had spent quite some time trying to figure it and her out.

Something was different today. There was a strength in Alex that hadn't been there the last time she was here but there was also something else.

Selena gave Alex's hand a squeeze and put the bottle on the

counter. "Eat something, you may not be quite human, but you will still succumb to that."

"I should be so lucky." Alex grumbled and poured herself another glass. Raising it up she called out to anyone who could hear. "A toast! TO LIFE!"

Selena cringed as the leprechauns in the corner booth laughed raucously.

A CHILL RAN up Selena's spine. Something was wrong. As one of the best Reapers in the business, Alex took lives. Now she was toasting them.

The irony was lost on no one in the bar and Selena watched as information and rumors started to circulate through the room.

"Oh Alex."

CHAPTER TWO
20 YEARS LATER

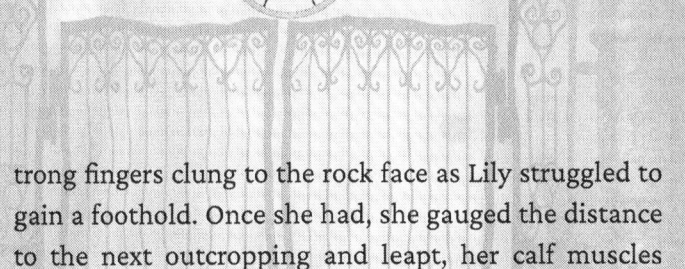

Strong fingers clung to the rock face as Lily struggled to gain a foothold. Once she had, she gauged the distance to the next outcropping and leapt, her calf muscles cramping as she pushed off with all her might reaching out for the jutting rock.

"Oof..."

First one hand, then the other got a good grip as she pulled herself up, forearms and shoulders straining with the effort. One slip and she was dead. A few more harrowing leaps and she crested the face of the cliff. Grunting with the exertion she finally pulled herself over and rolled onto her back exhausted.

For just a split-second Lily wondered why she did this to herself. A hand on her breast was all the reminder she needed.

She could feel the scar on her chest under her shirt as it moved along with her heartbeat. She was a thrill seeker, plain, but not simple.

Rolling onto her knees she stood up carefully.

The sky was a brilliant blue and she swore she could see past the horizon in this light. Free climbing was one of her favorite things to do, especially after a long work week, but it did push the limits of her thrill seeking. Pulling out her camera she took a few shots to capture the view and so she could refer to it later for her paintings.

The wind picked up and she leaned into it trying to keep her footing. The last thing she needed was to fall. She sat again and reached into her waist pack to pull out her windbreaker. Her sweat soaked shirt was chilling her to the bone. The plan had been to stay up on the ridge for another hour or so but if the wind continued, she would have to head down sooner.

Lily drew her knees up to her chest and hugged them tight, letting the emotions that had built up during the climb wash over her.

It was her twenty-year anniversary. Twenty years since her parents had been killed and she had become an orphan. Twenty years of wondering why she survived. Twenty years of feeling alone. The tears that fell were warm as they rolled down her face, but they scalded her soul.

Angry she wiped the tears away. It was unfair. She should have died with them that night, instead she'd been spared.

The scar on her chest reminded her every day how close she came to death that night. This climb today represented how close she now came every day.

Lily refused to live life in fear so she challenged death whenever and wherever she could. It probably wasn't the smartest way to live, but it was how she had chosen to. Needless to say, relationships were an afterthought since most couldn't keep up with her. It was a way of life she had resigned herself to.

"Enough wallowing Lil." She gave herself a shake and stood up.

Stretching carefully, she started to make her way along the ridge toward the walk off. It was about a quarter mile before the path and at least an hour's walk down, so she had plenty of time to get rid of the melancholic grip the day was having on her soul.

"How the hell does she keep getting away with it?" Basque crouched down and started doodling in the dirt. "The boss is going to be pissed."

Rowena Child was the second-best Reaper in the world, and she had fought her way to that spot by taking every job she could. She had an end goal, to be the best, but this one was her white whale. Having her protégé point out the obvious pissed her off.

She smacked him in the back of the head and stomped off. This was Alex's doing. She was sure of it.

How was it possible that this one person, this one human, had managed to avoid death for the past twenty years after coming so close in the first place?

Rowena had purposely bumped into Lily Heatherton at the base of the cliff. She wanted to get a feel for this woman. The last time she'd come across her had been twenty years before, when she had worked side by side with Alex Dante. Until that night. The night Lily Heatherton should have died.

The night had been a banner one for Reapers. Death had ordered that at least 50 families would die that night on top of the deaths that were scheduled. The Reaper with the most kills would not only be promoted but they would also be looked on with favor.

Alex Dante had been ruthless, going after families on the road and proving to Death himself why she was the best. When she backed off a kill though, Rowena hadn't understood and had decided to take the last car out herself. The fight they'd had that night had been dirty and physical resulting in the survival of one person. Lily Heatherton. Rowena was determined to find out why and how.

Alex Dante had long been Death's favorite Reaper, but not for much longer if Rowena had anything to say about it.

"Come on fool!" Rowena yanked Basque to his feet.

As a Reaper apprentice, he served her until she saw fit to let him act on his own or until he proved himself, as she had so many years ago with Alex.

She had some research to do and maybe, just maybe, she could put a bug in someone's ear about rectifying a twenty-year-old mistake and take out her competition in the process.

The image she had of Alex from that night was burned into her mind. She would make Alex pay for cutting her loose the way she did.

CHAPTER
THREE

Alex leaned against the rail as she watched Lily place her climbing gear in the back of her jeep. Twenty years. A long time for the woman she watched, a blink of an eye for Alex.

Never in all her time as a Reaper had she ever cared about the consequences. She never cared about who was left behind when she took someone. Never cared about the person whose life she snuffed out. But Lily...

There was something about her eyes that had captivated Alex all that time ago. A spark that no other human being she'd ever encountered had. She couldn't snuff it out. It felt wrong, ugly.

Twenty years ago, her own apprentice had tried to make a name for herself and took a kill. Alex had barely been able to stop her when she got to Lily.

Lily should have died that night and for all intents, Alex had thought she had.

The gaping wound in Lily's chest courtesy of Rowena's and

her battle had awoken something in Alex she still didn't understand.

She had run away to the Hotel that night in an attempt to drown her angst and sorrows.

It was Selena who had given her the news that her latest "kill" wasn't dead. Alex smiled, Selena reminded her of one of her old teachers, she had a way of knowing exactly what was going on and what you needed. So did the Hotel. She had left the Hotel after seven days refreshed, promoted, and determined to keep an eye on Lily Heatherton. And she had, for the past twenty years.

Now, she made a point of being present whenever Lily was doing something that would push the limits of life and limb. Lily was tempting fate and death and Alex knew better than anyone; Death did not like being tempted.

Lily slammed the trunk shut and spun around catching a glimpse of the woman she had seen at her last climb.

Frowning she watched as the tall woman spun on her heel and strode away, her long leather duster and dark hair flowing behind her. It was a bit warm to be wearing a jacket like that, even here, and again she wondered who the beautiful woman was.

The urge to follow her was strong, overpowering.

Let it go Lil. Her head was definitely trying to rule this decision, but her heart won out.

"Hey! Wait up!" Lily rushed after her and saw the woman's gait falter before picking up speed.

Alex cursed under her breath. The last thing she needed was to interact with a human without collecting a soul. Death would know.

"Please!" The plea in Lily's voice made Alex slow down.

Dammit. It was a coincidence, that's all, that's what she would say. Alex turned around.

"Can I help you?" Her husky voice dropped an octave as her eyes locked with Lily's.

Alex watched as Lily stopped short, suddenly seeming unsure. She could see the mark on Lily's chest and tried to look away. Lily brought a hand up unconsciously covering the scar before speaking.

"I've seen you before, haven't I? At another one of my climbs? I'm Lily, Lily Heatherton." Lily extended a hand and waited.

Alex hesitated before putting her hand out. The moment they touched Alex was jolted to her core. The contact should have been quick and unfeeling, instead it took her breath away as she felt awash in Lily's sorrow and what her parent's death meant to her.

She yanked her hand back and looked down at Lily. Alex could tell from the glazed look in Lily's eyes that she had felt something as well.

"Alex, Alex Dante. Look I have to go-" She walked off before Lily could say another word.

She needed a drink and some questions answered. Lily was tempted to go speak to her old teacher, but the changes at her alma mater, L'Academie, of late made that impossible for now, so her first choice was out.

Since she couldn't go there, there was only one other place to go, The Hotel.

Lily looked on as Alex walked away. *What just happened?* She considered following her but when she saw Alex go into the small stone building that housed the restrooms, she headed back to her jeep instead.

Lost in thought, she still made sure to go through her regular stretching routine to ease up some of the tightness she always experienced after a climb. Clasping her hands behind her back she stretched them out and glanced toward the small building one last time before getting in the car.

With both hands on the steering wheel she looked down at her right hand. It felt tingly after shaking Alex's hand. She shook it out and started the car, smiling as she thought about what she had seen in the other woman's eyes. Want.

CHAPTER FOUR

Alex walked through the restroom door and into the lobby of The Hotel Paranormal. One of her favorite things about the hotel was the access. She'd never been short an entry. Like all other entries to their realm, they were everywhere if you knew where to look. As a frequent customer and considering she'd been around for a long time, she knew more than some other beings.

Some of the newer vamps and shifters only had access to a couple of entries. Of course, that could be because they kept trying to bring in contraband, namely unwilling human 'guests'.

"Ms Dante!" Shy, mousy Ava was more animated than Alex had ever seen.

"What is it Ava?" Alex had given up trying to get the clerk to just call her Alex. Whenever she got excited, she reverted to formalities.

"You have a message." She handed Alex a folded piece of paper.

. . .

R is looking into your work dear. Hot on your heels I believe. She wants something you have and wants what you want. E

Alex looked around the lobby for the source of the note.

"Where is the one who gave this to you?"

She growled at Ava for the first time ever and immediately realized her mistake.

Ava practically folded in on herself as she tried to get away from her, fear flashing from her eyes. Cursing her behavior Alex tried to reach out to her. She wasn't at all surprised by the whimper from the other woman.

"Ava...Ava I'm sorry..." Alex was not the type of Reaper who liked to flaunt her abilities. She specifically tried never to use the tone she just used, unless she was working.

Ava drew herself up and swallowed. This job was not for the meek and normally she did quite well against most of the paranormal creatures that frequented the hotel but there were a few that frightened her to her core when they didn't abide by pleasantries. Shifters and Reapers.

Shifters were bad enough. Not the older ones of course but the young ones always thought it was funny to appear in their altered state. They took absolute pleasure in unsettling her. But with them it was mostly just appearance.

Reapers though. They had a tone they used before taking a life, an almost guttural growl that a person felt in their soul. It was generally the last sound a person heard, and it felt like air had rushed into your heart and it was about to burst out of your chest. It was a unique feeling, scary yet welcoming. That's what she had felt. With a slight nod to Alex, she headed back to the front desk, a shell of the person who had given Alex the note.

Cursing herself, Alex re-read the note before ripping it up. A chill ran down her spine as the implication of it hit her. Someone had seen her with Lily. Alex had no clue who E was, but she had no doubt about who R was. Rowena. They had crossed paths several times over the past twenty years, but they tended to give each other a wide berth. Now it seemed that was over.

She looked over at Ava and cringed as the woman jumped back startled when one of the vamps who had just come in tapped on the desk. The poor thing was white as a sheet. It would take her some time to get over the effect of Alex's voice on her.

She was about to go apologize again when she was grabbed firmly by the arm.

Hand raised she spun around to find herself face to face with Selena.

"Leave it alone Alex."

Alex's shock at seeing Selena outside the bar rendered her speechless. She allowed herself to be led into the bar and took a seat at the far counter.

"What just happened?" Alex flexed her arm and knew there would be bruises where Selena had grabbed her. It was an unnaturally strong grip and she looked at Selena through narrowed eyes.

"Stop looking at me like that. I was trying to make sure you didn't get yourself kicked out of here, there aren't too many places where you are welcome you know." Selena wiped her hands down and placed a small glass in front of each of them.

Reaching behind the large shelf at the bar Selena pulled out a crystal bottle filled with a bright green liquid. She poured a shot of the green liquor in each glass and waited for Alex to pick it up.

"Is this-"

"Yes, it's Dragon Whiskey, 200-year-old Dragon Whiskey to be exact."

"But that's impossible to get…" Alex shook her head. She felt dazed by everything that had transpired in the past thirty minutes.

"We need to talk." Selena downed the shot and smiled fiercely. It was rare for Selena to get involved in the affairs of others, at least directly, but this time she'd had no choice. Creatures were talking and there was something bad coming.

Alex gulped down the whiskey and started choking. It was by far the most potent drink she'd ever had. Most drinks didn't affect her at all but this…she could feel the warmth of it as it coursed through her body. Best of all she felt her body unwind, the tension and anxiety she had been feeling was gone.

"Wow." Her normally raspy voice was even more hoarse as the aftereffects of the liquor hung on.

"Yes wow." Selena's voice held a timbre Alex was not familiar with and when she looked into Alex's eyes, they flashed the same green as the whiskey.

Alex blinked but the flash was gone.

"You've talked to her, haven't you?" Selena had lowered her voice considerably.

"Who?"

"Don't give me who, dammit." Selena huffed. "You know exactly who I mean, the little girl."

"She's not a little girl anymore." The moment the words were out she tried to take them back.

"Uh huh…" Selena poured them each another shot of

Dragon Whiskey and put the bottle away carefully before turning back to the Reaper.

"Do you realize what will happen if-"

"I know! Don't you think I know? It's just. There is something about her I can't forget. When she touched my hand..." Alex's eyes darkened at the memory.

Selena didn't miss any of it.

"There is a rumor."

Alex glared at her. "What rumor?"

Selena considered her options. She generally tried to stay out of the affairs of anyone or anything that frequented the Hotel but every once in a while, she felt a compulsion to help, interfere, butt in, whatever anyone wanted to call it.

This was one of those times and it had started twenty years ago.

"Do you feel different Alex?"

"What?"

"Twenty years ago, there was a little girl whose life you couldn't take. You marked her and whether you know it or not you are linked to her."

Eyes black as coal glared at the bartender. "What the hell are you talking about Selena?"

CHAPTER FIVE

Lily threw her gear into the hallway closet and groaned as she arched her back. She had made great time getting back home but she should have spent some more time stretching before the long drive.

She felt stiff and her shoulders were tight from the climb so she made her way to the bedroom doorway so she could hang from her pull up bar. Gripping the bar firmly she let herself hang down smiling faintly as she heard her muscles and joints pop, relieving some of the tension.

Bringing her hands down she flexed her right hand again, the memory of the spark she had felt, while hours old, still fresh in her mind.

"Hmmm." Grabbing a bottle of water from the fridge she plopped down on the couch. The view from her climb still vivid in her mind's eye. The horizon and the play of light against the clouds had been breathtaking. She got up with a groan.

She needed to sketch it before it was gone from her mind. Lily was lucky enough to be able to make a living from her death-defying feats. The photos that she took and the paintings she made were in high demand. She had a way of capturing an instant in time along with the emotion that went with it.

Thirty minutes into her sketching she realized she had actually made two sketches. One was a quick sketch of the view she'd seen. She had thrown some color in there to capture the general hues. It was rough but it conveyed what she needed to finish it. That plus the pictures she had taken would help her recreate the moment.

The other sketch took her breath away. It was the mysterious woman she had met. Lily couldn't consciously remember sketching it at all as she considered the woman's eyes once again. Lily had captured every angle of her face, softening it just a bit with the hair that billowed around her face. Her breath caught in her chest. The woman was beautiful and terrifying. There was something about her eyes that scared her, but they also drew her in. She touched the sketch tenderly.

"Alex Dante" There was a hint of a smile on her face as she whispered her name, but there was no one there to see it.

Alex never heard Selena's response. A roaring in her ears was the only warning she had that something was wrong. That and the unfamiliar pain in her chest.

Selena cursed in a language that hadn't been heard aloud in over a thousand years as the best Reaper she had ever known collapsed in front of her.

She was thankful there was only one other creature in the bar, and they were busy putting away a huge jug of mead and half a pig. Selena shivered, she hated trolls. Luckily though they were single minded, so it didn't seem to have noticed Alex collapse.

She came around the bar trying to figure out how to move her when Max, one of the hotel's employees, walked in. With a knowing smile, she let the big man pick Alex up and move her to the back of the bar where the seating area was. The couch he put her on automatically adjusted to her height.

"Thank you, Max." Selena patted him on the arm and smiled sweetly at him.

"Ms Selena." The timbre of his voice matched his stature, at almost seven feet tall he was an imposing figure. "Will there be anything else ma'am?"

Selena heard Alex stirring and shook her head.

"No, we should be fine." Turning back to Alex, she watched as the Reaper clutched unconsciously at her chest.

Nausea washed over Alex when she opened her eyes. Closing them tight, she waited another moment before opening them again and fixing her gaze on Selena. She welcomed Selena's help when she tried to sit up.

"What happened?" Alex's voice was barely a croak.

Selena kneeled in front of her and took her hands. "I told you. Connected. You touched her, didn't you?"

Alex could only nod.

"You connected twenty years ago, and you reconnected today."

"No, no, this doesn't make any sense, I'm a Reaper I can't, I don't-"

"Feel? Connect? Of course you can, and you do, just differently until now." Selena paused, "It's not allowed Alex."

"I know! You think I don't know that?" Alex jumped to her feet and grabbed the edge of the couch as she faltered. "This isn't happening, this can't be happening."

She paced in front of the bartender for a bit before stopping abruptly. "They know."

Selena nodded. "I think so. Well, at least one knows."

"Rowena...wait, Ava gave me a note." She closed her eyes and recited the words she'd read.

R is looking into your work dear. Hot on your heels I believe. She wants something you have and wants what you want. E

She recited it verbatim and looked questioningly at the bartender.

"Do you know who E is?"

Selena seemed to hesitate before shaking her head. "I don't, but we both know who R has to be. You need to stay away from Rowena."

Alex knew she was right, but the note worried her. It wasn't explicit or exact in any way, but she knew it had something to do with Lily.

"I need to go to work." Her tone was brusque and not at all grateful, but she didn't know how else to be now.

"Go." Selena waved her toward the door but stopped her as she passed. "Be careful."

Alex nodded and headed out. She didn't understand what was happening to her but for the first time since she had become a Reaper, Alex Dante was scared.

CHAPTER
SIX

Lily hung up the phone and smiled. Her agent was in love with the picture and sketch she had sent her. Not the sketch of Alex of course. She wanted to keep that one to herself.

She looked through the digital images of the view on her camera and stopped.

"What the..."

Zooming in she huffed when she still couldn't get a good look and gave up, choosing instead to connect her camera to her laptop for a better view of the pics.

Scrolling through she stopped at the picture in question. There was an unnatural haze on the right edge of her horizon. She zoomed in and froze.

"No, that's impossible." She looked at all of the other pictures but none of them showed what that one did.

The haze wasn't a haze at all. It was a faded image of her. It made absolutely no sense.

She carefully checked the exposure on her camera and inspected her lenses. There was nothing wrong with them. She looked at the image again and couldn't stop the involuntary gasp that escaped her. It was her all right, but it was distorted. Ugly. She shuddered. It shouldn't be there.

The sound of the doorbell almost knocked her off her chair.

"Easy Lil..." She looked at her watch wondering who could be at the door.

The package sitting in front of her door was small and nondescript, no bigger than a box of matches. Wrapped in brown paper, the only words visible were her name.

"Hmmm..." Lily picked it up and looked up and down the hallway. No one had buzzed to let her know there was a package for her. Already unsettled from the image of herself in the pictures she took, she placed the little package on the table by the front door. She was curious but spooked, she would deal with it later.

She went back to her photos. It wasn't the first time something strange had shown up in her pictures. There had been an ominous haze or two that had appeared on a few of her photos, but this was the first time she could see herself in it.

She opened her photo editing software, but she already knew she would be unable to remove it.

Funny though, these were the images that sold the best according to her agent. "They called to people." She'd said.

"Hmm...they don't call to me that's for sure." She spent ten more minutes trying and gave up. The other photos didn't bother her so much, but this one, it was of her for goodness sakes.

Enough Lil. She closed her laptop and headed to her bedroom. She needed to shower and take a quick nap. Thanks to her friend Rosslyn, she had a blind date to get ready for. She lamented ever having said she would go, but she'd promised.

The mysterious little package still called to her, but she was already running late.

"I'll deal with you tomorrow." She muttered.

Alex's face was the last thing the old man saw. When she stepped back, she took the time to look around. The room at the hospice was decorated so that the old man would be comfortable, with all the comforts of home and yet, he was alone when she took him.

"Someone should have been with you." Her voice gruff with emotion, Alex could not shake the feeling of melancholy that had gripped her since she showed up for him.

She recognized the old man. She had been the one to take his wife just a few short years before. His prayers had angered her at the time.

Instead of asking for his wife's life, he had prayed for her death to free her from the pain she was in. She didn't understand it.

Alex had been tempted then to show herself to him and ask him why he would ever ask for death to come for his wife.

Now was her chance.

"Why?" She asked.

The old man gave her a sympathetic smile and one word as he walked toward the light Alex had shown him.

"Love."

Confused, she was about to leave when she felt the call again. Another life, another soul. It never bothered her before, except for the one night twenty years ago, but it bothered her now.

Snap out of it Alex.

Without another thought, she turned her back on him and headed down to the emergency room where a family of three was waiting.

Rowena went through the archives slowly, page by page. Some things never changed and even though the use of electronic devices was now sanctioned, Les Archives de Mort were kept and maintained in print.

Basque brushed his hair back from his eyes and glanced at his mentor. She was fixated on Death's favorite reaper, Alexandra Dante.

He didn't know the whole story, but he knew enough. Enough to know that the battle brewing between the two of them would benefit him most of all.

"What are we looking for again?"

"Anything that shows that Dante let anyone go. Even a hint of it." Rowena practically growled at him and he winced.

"Okay but wouldn't someone know? Wouldn't Death?"

"No... Alex is clever and with far more friends than any Reaper should have. Something is not right and I'm going to find out what it is. When I do, Lily Heatherton is mine."

With a shrug of his shoulders, Basque continued looking. His book covered the eighteenth century and was as big as the table he sat at. This was going to take forever.

Lily smiled to hide her grimace. Not only was she tired, but the date was a huge disaster thus far. Her friend Rosslyn had decided that they should go on a double date. Rosslyn's date, Ben, was perfect for her friend, with the same temperament and sense of humor.

Unfortunately, the person Rosslyn had fixed Lily up with was more than a bit forward, with a sense of humor leaning toward bathroom humor and, he was a guy. Lily sighed as Rosslyn winked at her.

Try as she might, none of her friends could understand that she truly had no real interest in men. And for right now, women either. She didn't have time for all the drama that was a part of any relationship.

The only person in the past year who had sparked any kind of interest in her was Alex Dante.

"Hey…hey!" Her date, Braxton James, nudged her. "Where'd ya go? Did you hear anything I said?"

"Hmm…sure, I'm sorry. I'm just tired, I had a tough climb today I wasn't expecting to go out tonight."

"Yeah, yeah, you climb hills and stuff." Braxton leaned back in his chair and tried to look sexy and knowledgeable at the same time. It didn't work.

"Cliffs, mountains, I even do some rappelling. It is not, hills and stuff." Her tone made him sit up sharply and Rosslyn shook her head at her, pleading.

"Isn't that the same thing?" He leaned in toward her. "Why do you do that stuff anyway? Rosslyn says you make money from that, but I don't see how."

"I'm sure you don't."

Rosslyn put her hand on his. "Now, now…we're supposed to be having dinner and getting to know each other, not questioning motives or career choices."

That was enough for her.

"Look, I really have had a long day. It was really nice to meet you, but I don't think this is going to work. Roz I'll call you tomorrow."

He grabbed her hand when she got up to leave.

"Hey, I thought…you know. We were getting on okay and all." He smiled, trying to be nice, but his eyes were hard.

A chill ran up her back at the look in his eyes. She pulled her hand back and grabbed her jacket. "Tomorrow Roz."

Lily smiled grimly at her friend as Rosslyn mouthed back. *I'm sorry.*

By the time Lily got to her apartment she had pretty much put the horrible evening behind her. She would have a heart to heart with her friend tomorrow about the failed blind date, with explicit instructions to never do that to her again.

Kicking off her shoes, she peeled off her dress, enjoying the feel of the cool air in the apartment on her bare skin. The scar on her chest the only thing marring the view.

Pouring herself a glass of wine she sat on the couch tucking her legs under her and reached for the sketch she'd made of Alex. She didn't like doing portraits normally, but she was quite pleased with this one. The woman was gorgeous.

Lily took a sip and smiled. She had another climb in about ten days, with any luck she would see her again.

"Who are you Alex Dante?"

CHAPTER
SEVEN

Loud banging jolted Lily out of a sound sleep. She'd been dreaming about Alex and even now the lower half of her body still felt warm.

Grabbing her robe, she made her way to the door. Passing the hallway table, she stopped for a moment ignoring the banging. The small package was exactly where she had left it. Without a thought as to why, she took it and put it in her pocket. The pounding on the door continued.

"What the...Who is it?" She was about to unlock the door but stopped when she got no answer.

"Hello?"

Lily jumped back when the banging started again.

"I'm going to call the police!"

Silence.

After a few minutes, she peeked through the peephole. The hallway was empty.

She wanted to open the door but without knowing who was out there, she was scared to.

When the doorbell rang, she cursed out loud, hand to her chest.

"Who is it?" Looking through the peephole again she was surprised to see Braxton. She cursed under her breath before opening the door.

"Jesus Christ, Braxton, it's three in the morn-"

Braxton grabbed her around the throat and slammed her into wall.

"You're a bitch you know that?" His words slurred and he reeked of alcohol.

Lily fought against the dark spots that filled her vision and tried to focus. When he slammed her against the wall again, she grabbed his wrists trying to absorb the blow.

"Brax...ton...stop..." His hands were like a vice around her neck.

With all the strength she could muster she twisted in his grip and slammed her elbow down across his forearms forcing him to let her go. Off balance he fell into the wall as she dropped to the floor. Scrambling away from him she grabbed her phone from the table and dialed 911 even as he came at her again. Her foot caught him squarely between his legs.

"911 what is your emergency?"

Lily didn't have a chance to answer. Braxton sprang at her from his knees and slammed his elbow into her chest.

"No!" Alex doubled over in her room at the Hotel and in the blink of an eye, she was gone.

Alex stood behind the man as he raised his hand to strike Lily again. The rage that filled her was unlike any emotion she had ever felt. Without a thought, she grabbed him by the nape of his neck and tossed him backwards into the wall not even looking to see the aftermath.

Lily lay still as death, looking like nothing less than a broken doll.

"Lily."

Alex went down on her knees beside her. She hesitated before touching the scar on her breast, ignoring the jolt she felt. She grimaced as the skin under her hand grew hot and Lily took a deep rasping breath. Alex could see the beginnings of a bruise around Lily's neck and turned to look at the man who had put it there.

He wasn't slated to die. She wasn't under contract for him either, but the urge to take his life was overwhelming. Braxton James. Death would know.

Reapers walked a fine line between fate and folly. It was possible for someone to pay for someone's death, but most were fated, though lately... Alex wanted nothing more than to end his life right there.

The sound of sirens stopped her. Lily would have enough questions to answer. With Lily beginning to stir and the authorities approaching, Alex decided it would be best if she wasn't there. She placed a gentle kiss on her forehead and said goodbye.

"Take care Lily." She had no idea how she had known something was wrong with Lily, or what she herself was feeling, but she knew someone who might.

Lily opened her eyes just as Alex shimmered away.

"Alex?"

CHAPTER
EIGHT

Lily grabbed her robe and brushed off Rosslyn's help.

"Come on Lil, I said I was sorry."

"Sorry?" Her voice was a hoarse whisper, the bruising around her throat making it hard to talk. "Where the hell did you find that guy?"

Roz wrung her hands and paced. The police had called her when they'd discovered her cell number on both Lily's and Braxton's phones. It had taken some persuading for Lily to even talk to her when she had gotten to the emergency room.

"He's Ben's friend."

The emergency room was crazy busy and loud. Lily was grateful to be getting released at just after eight in the morning.

"Yeah well, he almost killed me, the drunken ass." Lily had been trying to sit up when the police had gotten to her apartment.

She'd been shocked at their appearance and even more shocked when she had seen an unconscious Braxton being checked out by another officer.

Thankfully, her own injuries had kept the questions to a minimum. That and the smell of alcohol that emanated from Braxton left little doubt in the officer's mind as to what appeared to have transpired.

With Braxton arrested and herself checked out in the emergency room, she could reflect now on what she had seen. Not what, who.

"Are you sure you're okay to go home? I mean, they had you hooked up to all sorts of stuff when I got here." Lily could see how anxious Roz was at finding her like that and softened.

"It was a precaution Roz, I'm fine. Sore and hurting, but fine." Lily put on her robe and the slippers Roz had bought her. "Please, just take me home."

Roz couldn't hide the hurt look on her face. "Sure, of course. Let me check on those release papers."

Alex paced in front of the bar and waited for Selena to finish up with the group of shifters who had come in. She had ignored two calls already this morning allowing other reapers to do her job, but she had questions. Thankfully she didn't have long to wait.

"What did you do Alex?"

"I don't know…I don't know what's wrong with me." Emotions were uncoiling inside of her. Emotions that she wasn't familiar with.

By the time she finished explaining everything that happened, Selena was pacing.

"Well, that certainly ties into what I overheard."

"Overheard?" Alex didn't like the sound of it.

"Rowena is looking through everything you've ever done."

"What?" Alex's tone changed and Selena just waved it away.

"Don't use that tone on me love, it doesn't work." Selena gave her a pat and escorted her to the door. "You need to make a decision before the call goes out."

"What call?"

Selena shook her head and gave her a gentle shove. "Follow your heart."

"But...I don't know how."

It took less than a day.

Someone had escaped Death once again and this time Death had taken notice. According to a fellow Reaper also staying at the Hotel, a young woman in San Francisco was now a primary target. She had cheated death on numerous occasions, most recently just a day or two before.

Add to that, information provided by a Reaper in the New York City area who had seen several images in a gallery, that had somehow managed to capture death in different incarnations. The images appeared almost as a double exposure but the Reaper knew what he was looking at and had reported back.

The Reaper they reported to? Rowena Child. It hadn't taken her long to trace the photos back to the same young woman.

The hunt was on now for this woman who continued to cheat death and had the nerve to capture him on film. Like that infamous night twenty years prior, the reward for collecting this soul was boundless. But Death had put some specific rules in place. It had to be a death worth recording. The archives were full of people who had tried to defy death and as a result had died spectacularly. Those that Death didn't give a thought to just died and were forgotten.

This time though Death wanted the soul delivered directly to him.

ALEX FLUNG her glass at the wall and reveled in watching it explode into tiny pieces. Lily was marked for death and there was nothing she could do. In less than eight days the Reapers would be free to go after her, with the rise of the Harvest Moon. Her sources told her that Rowena was chomping at the bit to be the one to bring Lily before Death.

Her duster billowed behind her as she paced in front of the immense picture window in her room.

"I can fix this...I can fix this..."

What she felt for this woman was foreign to her. She cared, and in doing so she was tempting the wrath of Death himself.

Alex needed to keep Lily safe but to do that would expose them both.

"Dammit!"

She dropped down onto a chair and realized that for the first time in her existence, she didn't know what to do.

CHAPTER NINE

Lily looked in the mirror and inspected the ugly bruise around her throat. Tying a scarf around her neck, she did her best to disguise it before heading out. Two days' rest had done her good, but she was starting to get cabin fever. Besides, she was on a mission.

When she had finally gotten home from the hospital, she had been in desperate need of a shower. Taking off her robe, she had once again found the small package that had been left at her door. Ripping off the wrapping she had opened the box to find a card, a plain card with only one thing on it, an address. She was curious and determined to find out what it meant.

She hesitated at the door before heading out. The attack a few days prior still vivid in her mind. Determined, she faced her fear of opening the door.

Come on Lil. She looked down at the card. The address wasn't far, just a twenty minute or so drive. "Let's go see what this means."

Alex hung back and waited while Lily parked her Jeep, she had no intention of letting herself be spotted again. Her breath caught in her throat when Lily finally stepped out.

She was more beautiful than Alex had ever seen her. Her light brown hair whipped around her head, blonde highlights catching in the sun while the trench coat she wore accentuated her every curve. Letting out her breath she watched as Lily headed down toward a small maintenance building.

Reapers were always hungry for a good kill and anything that bought them favor with Death was a definite plus. Six days. Alex had six days to save her, but she still had no idea how.

Curiosity brought her out in the open when she saw Lily look down at a card in her hand. The building she was headed to was one of many doorways to the Hotel Alex was aware of.

A glint of light made her look away and that was when she saw her. Rowena was sitting on a bench watching as Lily approached. Rowena caught her eye and when she smiled, Alex caught a glimpse of her true face. Fear drove her to do the unspeakable.

"No!" The moment the words were out of her mouth Alex regretted it. She watched as Lily stopped and turned, recognition dawning in her eyes.

"Alex?" Lily hesitated. She brought a hand up to her chest allowing Alex to feel her anxiety and fear.

Alex glared at Rowena. She couldn't hide her connection now. Rowena would make sure of it. When she shimmered away, Alex knew there was no going back.

She strode up to Lily, grabbed her by the hand and started walking toward the small building.

"Wait a minute! What the hell, you can't just-

"Quiet!" Alex barely managed to temper her tone as she stopped walking. "Where were you going?"

Lily shoved the card in her face. "Someone left me this."

Alex took the card and saw, not just the address where they were, but something more. Barely noticeable in the corner of the card was the Hotel's logo. Someone had sent Lily an invitation.

Alex knew the rules. A human had to enter the Hotel willingly. This was especially helpful with some of the younger carnivores who liked to show their dinner a good time before dispensing with them. Her decision was easy. Six days.

"Do you want to go in?"

"What?"

Alex loosened her grip on Lily's hand and whispered. "Do you want to go in?"

Lily tried to understand what she was feeling. Her heart was beating erratically as she absorbed the initial charge she felt when Alex took her hand. Looking into her eyes she saw more than want. She saw a smoldering desire and a hint of…fear. Fear of what?

Not trusting herself to speak, she merely nodded.

"Trust me?" Alex said.

Alex's husky voice sent a shiver down her spine. She had no idea where they were going but right now, in this moment, she didn't care.

"Yes."

Lily let herself be led to the nondescript door behind the building. She couldn't believe she was doing this. She may be a thrill seeker, but she had never done anything like this.

She took a step back when Alex opened the door, unsure and there was a moment of panic when Alex stepped over the threshold into the dimly lit room. She briefly wondered if she was making a terrible mistake.

A reassuring squeeze of her hand was all she needed to follow Alex through the door.

ALEX APPRECIATED Lily's expression as she took in the opulence of the Hotel's lobby. Six days. She had six days to figure out how to save her and it occurred to her when she saw Rowena that maybe the Hotel was the place to do so.

"Come on." Alex escorted her to the front desk and touched the bell. When Ava came out from the back room her eyes darkened briefly when she saw Alex.

Alex sighed, she still had a lot to make up for with her.

"Ms Dante and...?"

"Ava, this is Lily, Lily Heatherton. She's going to need a room for a couple of days."

"Wait...what?" Lily turned on Alex. "Where the hell are we?"

Alex ignored Ava's raised eyebrows at the question.

"You said you trusted me. Will you trust me when I say that you need a room here for a couple of days?"

"A couple of-" Lily looked around again at the empty lobby. "One night."

"Done." She took the key Ava handed her. "Come on."

CHAPTER
TEN

"Dammit!" Alex couldn't contain her frustration as she stopped outside Lily's room. *Had it only been an hour?*

When Lily had let herself into her room, Alex's exclamation had surprised her. The room was Alex's. She'd made a point of leaving Lily in the room while she went back to talk to the front desk.

Try as she might and no matter how much she argued with them, the room the Hotel kept assigning to Lily was her own.

The tension between them was palpable when she finally stepped inside. Lily had made herself a bit more comfortable, taking off her coat and scarf, but that was it. Alex couldn't help but stare at the bruise around her neck, wishing once again that she had ended that bastard Braxton's life.

"You're staring." Lily said quietly.

"Sorry." Alex looked away and took off her own coat, tossing the duster onto the bed before she sat down.

"You must have a lot of questions." It wasn't a question, just a statement of fact as she waited for the onslaught from Lily.

Lily tore her eyes away from Alex and looked down at her hands. She felt like a fish out of water. Nothing felt familiar to her except Alex and that made absolutely no sense to her, she didn't know this woman.

Alex had taken Lily's breath away when she walked in. She exuded power and strength, her wild hair punctuating every movement she made. Her light olive skin against the black clothes she wore made her seem dangerous as well. Lily could feel the heat in Alex's gaze when she caught her staring. It felt like she was looking into her very soul.

"Who are you and where are we?"

"We are at a place we all call The Hotel."

"I think I'm going to regret asking, but who is 'we all'?"

Lily was surprised when Alex got up and started to pace.

"Do you believe Lily?"

"Believe what?"

"Do you believe in things that might not make sense?"

"Are you serious?" One look at her face told her Alex was being exactly that. "Well, I don't know if I quite understand what you're asking but I like to think I have an open mind."

"Fair enough."

Alex took that as permission and shimmered away only to reappear behind her.

"Turnaround."

The slap was unexpected, Lily's reaction wasn't, as she pushed her away and took a step back.

"What the hell are you?"

"My name is Alexandra Dante and I'm a Reaper."

"Reaper? Like the Grim Reaper?" She grabbed at her neck. "This is a dream, right? I'm still in the hospital?"

Alex grabbed both of her hands and placed one over the scar on Lily's chest.

"This is no dream Lily. Hear me out. Let me explain and if I don't answer your questions, you can leave, okay? Please?"

Lily nodded. The spark she'd felt at their first meeting had happened again when Alex had touched her scar. This was nuts, it couldn't be real.

"It is Lily."

"It is what?"

"Real."

Alex had no idea if Lily believed anything she had told her but when she insisted on seeing the lobby again she wasn't about to fight her on it.

Lily stopped just shy of the lobby, but a gentle nudge from Alex encouraged her to keep walking.

It was busy now and Alex watched as Lily's eyes opened in wonderment when she saw the creatures who now inhabited it. The leprechauns at the front desk were busy trying to wrangle freebies from Ava while Max dealt with a shape shifter who seemed determined to try and intimidate the seven-foot-tall desk clerk.

"Are you sure this is real Alex?" Her voice was a whisper.

Alex took her hand. "It is." She smiled when Lily gave her hand a squeeze.

A menacing chuckle interrupted the moment.

"Well, well...looky here, Dante's got a human with her." The gravelly voice was all too familiar to Alex.

"Maddox...Jax..." The men were a bit larger than Alex and her response was immediate as she pulled Lily closer to her. She kept a close eye on both Weres as they sniffed around Lily. They belonged to a particularly vicious pack that took absolute pleasure in rocking the boat for other paranormals with their behavior, flaunting their abilities in the human world.

"You slumming Alex?" Jax, the younger of the two had more balls than brains.

"I'm escorting a guest around; do you need something?"

"Oh, I need something all right." Maddox came up behind Lily and breathed in her scent. "Yum"

Lily felt his breath on her neck and shoved him. "Back off!"

Jax laughed rubbing his hands together. "Feisty."

Lily took a step back when his features rippled, revealing the wolf beneath the human facade. "What the f-"

Alex slammed a palm into his chest sending him crashing into the fountain and prepared herself for Maddox.

Palms raised Maddox backed up. Alex's eyes were like black onyx and he knew they had pushed the reaper too far. "Whoa...no harm...just taking a little taste."

HE WATCHED Alex take her human by the hand and walk into the bar. It was no skin off his nose but in all his years, he'd never known a Reaper to bring a human to the Hotel. Hell, he'd never seen a Reaper *be* with a human whose life they weren't taking.

Laughing he helped his brother pull himself out of the fountain.

"What the hell are you laughing at?" Jax growled as he pulled at his wet clothes.

"Hmm? Oh, just that I've never seen anything get under Dante's skin like that before." He saw everyone's eyes follow them into the bar. "If it was a secret, it sure isn't anymore."

THE SHIFT from the airy open feel of the lobby to the darkened emotion laden ambience of the bar was jarring. Old timers didn't even notice it anymore, but Lily did. The bar had an old world feel to it. It reminded her of a bar she had visited in the Czech Republic a year ago. Even the barkeep was old world with her long dress and makeup.

What the hell had she gotten herself into?

Alex could sense her hesitation and pulled her along gently. There weren't too many humans who had ever frequented the hotel much less the bar, for a good reason. It wasn't meant for them, but it didn't take long for Lily to adjust.

"Why did he smell me? His face changed? What was he?" Lily's rapid-fire questions were going to make her head explode so Alex did the only thing she could think of.

She kissed her.

Alex was certainly no virgin. Having lived more lifetimes than she could remember there were times when she sought solace and sexual release with other beings, but this was different. For the first time in her existence, she felt whole.

When Lily deepened the kiss, she followed suit, feeling more than she had ever felt in her lifetime.

Lily's flare of anger died the moment she felt Alex's lips on hers. There was no longer any sadness or melancholy, there was just Alex. Her head was telling her to stop but her heart wanted more and when she responded in kind, Alex's response made her heart soar. Right now, in that bar, no one else existed.

The sound of someone clearing their throat made them both jump.

"Selena." Alex was almost sheepish when she looked at the other woman. She had done the exact opposite of what Selena had advised her to do.

"What have you done Alex?"

Selena stormed past them and into the back-meeting room, slamming the door on its patrons.

The silence in the bar in the wake of the slammed door was deafening.

"Selena...wait!"

"Alex?"

In a moment of clarity Alex finally took in the audience in the bar who had watched their performance, focusing on the two reapers at the far table who raised their glasses. Lily appeared to be in shock about it all which was understandable. Between the unexpected kiss and what she had seen so far, Alex was certain she didn't know what to think.

"Merde! Come on!" She pulled Lily along with her and followed Selena into the back room. She still had six days to save Lily and she knew she couldn't do that without Selena's help.

Selena was pacing in front of the fireplace when Alex and Lily came through the door.

"Sit, sit."

She waited until they were settled, neither saying a word, before tossing an ancient manuscript at Alex.

"Read it."

Keeping an eye on the girl, Selena watched as understanding dawned on Alex's face.

"Now do you understand Alex?" She kneeled in front of her. "You can't save her."

"No." Alex shook her head violently and grabbed Lily's hand, content with the feeling it gave her. "I have time."

Selena nodded solemnly and showed them the door.

"No, you don't."

CHAPTER ELEVEN

Lily kicked the chair and stormed around the room. Alex hadn't said more than two words to her since taking her back to the room and ordering her not to leave.

"How dare she? I mean really, who the hell does she think she is?" Talking to herself in the mirror probably wasn't the sanest thing to do but she was stuck where she was for now. She had no idea what magic Alex had worked but she couldn't get the hell out of the room no matter how hard she tried.

A knock at the door stopped her frantic pacing.

"Hello?"

The miniature bellhop who opened the door was balancing a silver tray in one hand and keys in the other.

"Hello Miss... Ms Alex sent this up for you." He placed the tray on the small bench at the end of the bed and handed her a note.

"From Ms. Alex." With a small bow, he excused himself.

Curiosity got the better of her and she lifted the domed lid on the tray. The wonderful smells that came from the meal in front of her momentarily let her forget where she was. She slammed the lid down and read the note.

Dear Lily,

You said you trusted me. I am asking you to trust me again. I want to apologize for just abandoning you this way, but I need to keep you safe. I know I haven't given you the whole story yet, but I need you to know this basic truth. Your life is in danger. I know that you are probably thinking that your life is always in danger given the nature of what you do, but you're wrong. This danger is different. I promise I will explain everything when I get back. The staff at the Hotel has been instructed to give you whatever you need.

"I need to get out of here." She muttered as she continued to read.

They cannot and will not allow you to leave. You entered with me and you must leave with me. Try to get some rest, I know you are not fully recovered from the attack on you.

Give me this small amount of time to find some answers and explain. Trust me.

Alex

P.S. I cannot stop thinking about our kiss. There was a connection there that ~~made me feel~~...I will see you shortly. A

Her anger momentarily abated, Lily plopped down on the bed and re-read the last sentence. She smiled where she saw Alex had scratched out what she had written. Touching her lips, she could still imagine Alex's supple lips on hers. The feeling made her heart flutter.

"What the hell have you gotten yourself into Lily?"

ALEX READ through the old manuscript again and tried to find something, anything, that would help her save Lily.

She poured herself another drink and gulped it down not giving a damn about the murmuring behind her. The looks from some of the beings in the bar when she'd walked back in had ranged from pity to utter happiness. There were few paranormal beings who connected with humans on a regular basis. Sure, there were some who had, but the happy endings were few and far between.

Alex read the passage that Selena had highlighted again and slammed the manuscript shut. It was a stupid prophecy. She was sure that it couldn't be referring to her, but the evidence was beginning to suggest otherwise.

They will be marked at death by the harbinger of death.
The harbinger will not know peace
The marked one will die at the hand of death
The harbinger will have their release

THERE HAD TO BE A WAY. Two reapers had already tipped their hat to her and one of the leprechauns she'd seen earlier had made it a point to tell her that Basque was in the hotel. Rowena's smarmy little minion was already making inquiries about any human guests that might be staying there.

She touched her lips, a ghost of a smile on her face. The letter she'd written to Lily had been unexpected. She didn't write anybody, ever, but she needed to try to explain and it was all she could think of at the time.

Stop lying to yourself Alex. It wasn't her only recourse, but she wasn't ready to face her or her questions. With any luck, Lily would be asleep when she got back to the room. She would have to explain eventually, if only to keep Lily from trying to leave tomorrow.

By the time Alex got back to her room several hours later, she was exhausted.

Maddox had made a sly comment about Lily in the bar and for just the second time in her existence, Alex had gotten into a bar brawl.

Creatures readily took sides and it wasn't until Selena had appeared that everyone calmed down.

Selena's appearance created a lull that Maddox capitalized on and he got in a clean shot. There were certain rules at the Hotel that everyone was expected to follow. One of the most important rules? Respect of each other's abilities was paramount. It was just a split second, but in that moment, just as with the human who attacked Lily, Alex contemplated taking a life. And Selena knew it.

With Max's gentle enforcement, the beings involved including the erstwhile fae watching from the corner, set things right at the bar. Maddox had been pulled aside by Selena and when he left, his tail was literally between his legs.

Alex was a different matter. As a Reaper, she was automatically granted a special authority, but she had over stepped in her thoughts and Selena had pounced on it.

"What were you thinking?" She hissed.

"I wasn't obviously." Alex moved the small bag of ice and touched her cheek, the swelling making her wince.

"You can be asked to leave. *She* will be asked to leave."

Alex paced in front of the bar liked a caged animal. "I just need time. I can figure this out."

"You have less than six days Alex."

The bag of ice exploded when she slammed it down on the bar. "You think I don't know that!"

Alex had stalked out of the bar after her outburst without another word and now here she was, standing outside of her own room wondering if she was ready for what was on the other side.

CHAPTER TWELVE

She tried to be quiet as she let herself in.

The relief she felt when she caught sight of Lily in her bed changed to pure wonder.

Lily was laying across the bed sound asleep. She had changed out of her clothes and was wearing one of Alex's shirts as a nightshirt.

The sight of a vulnerable Lily wearing her shirt and lying in her bed produced an unfamiliar feeling in Alex's chest. Reapers don't feel like humans do, but in that instant, Alex Dante, Death's most loyal Reaper, understood what it felt like to love.

LILY FELT Alex sit on the edge of the bed and kept her eyes closed. She had starting to worry that she'd been abandoned but common sense had won out. Alex wouldn't abandon her. Granted, she couldn't know that for certain, but she did trust her, no matter who or what she was.

Lily shivered as Alex's fingers brushed the scar on her breast. Her touch was electric, and she felt it to her core.

"What are you doing?" Her voice was breathless as Alex's hand lingered.

"Hmm...oh sorry." Alex took her hand away and avoided her eyes.

Lily heard a tone she wasn't familiar with from Alex, uncertainty.

She reached over and turned on the light, gasping at the sight that greeted her. Alex's clothes were disheveled, her hair was wild and the visible swelling on her left cheek made Lily wince.

She touched Alex's cheek tenderly. "What happened?"

Alex grabbed her hand and gazed into her eyes. Lily swallowed nervously at what she saw in their dangerous depths.

"Ale-" Her words were smothered by Alex's lips on hers. The crushing brutality of it frightened and thrilled her. She relished the possessiveness of the kiss not caring one bit what was behind it. Lily lived life on the edge and loved it, this felt no different.

She could feel her heart pounding frantically as it tried to escape her chest, the sensations pulsing through her body were more than anything she had ever felt before with anyone.

Alex released her lips. "Tell me you feel it too." Her husky voice gave Lily goosebumps.

She nodded. Whatever was going on, whoever Alex was, none of that mattered right now.

She took Alex's hand and placed it over the scar, shivering as it brushed her breast.

"I do."

Rowena looked around Lily's apartment and couldn't hold back a smile. That idiot Braxton had been easy to control and had been easily convinced to go after Lily Heatherton. There was a darkness in him that he hadn't known about and Rowena had taken pleasure in unlocking it.

She could sense the residue of Lily's life force, but she could also feel Alex's presence in the apartment as she walked around.

Death always left a mark. Be it Death himself or one of his Reapers.

Basque had been unable to confirm the rumor that Alex had brought a human to the hotel, but Rowena didn't doubt it, given that Lily's apartment was vacant in the middle of the night. The perverse pleasure she felt at unsettling Alex the previous afternoon had been quite satisfying.

She stopped her stroll through the room at Lily's desk when she saw the sketch of Alex. Shock washed over her. Somehow, this human had captured the very essence of the Reaper. Beautiful, fiery, deadly.

Anger raged through her as she snatched the sketch up and started to tear it in half before stopping herself.

Without another thought she folded it and put it in her pocket.

Twenty years ago, Alex and she had set off on different trajectories. Alex had cast her aside for doing her job. She'd chosen a human over her own kind, over her.

"And the bitch had still been rewarded" She muttered.

Death had a soft spot for Alex. Always had. This was different though. Even Alex couldn't be so blatant about breaking the rules. Now, with a bit of subtle nudging on her part, this Lily Heatherton was a primary target. A human blatantly defying Death. She wasn't happy about having to wait to take the woman's life, but Death's rules had to be followed.

Lily Heatherton would be hunted down but Rowena had every intention of being the one to bring the woman before Death. He wanted her brought before him, but he didn't state what kind of condition she needed to be in.

CHAPTER
THIRTEEN

Alex lay on her side watching the rise and fall of Lily's chest with fascination. This woman had almost died just a few days ago, been thrust into a situation she had no familiarity with, and she was sleeping.

She envied her ability to sleep. As a Reaper, Alex didn't require sleep per se, but she did need rest and a chance to recharge. What happened between them had done more to recharge her than any amount of rest could have. Lily had succumbed to her just as readily as Alex had succumbed to Lily.

Their kiss had been brutal, but their actions afterward had been beyond tender. Lily had allowed her to explore every part of her body and Alex had relished it. She had stopped at her throat, the bruise vivid even in the semi darkness, but Lily had urged her on. Their exploration of each other had filled Alex with wonder and had lasted for some time. The connection between them, undeniable.

The feelings she had for this woman confused her though. Alex thought back to the old man and what he had said when she asked him why he had prayed for his wife's death. She was beginning to understand.

Seeing Lily lying on the floor of her apartment with that man ready to strike her again had done something to her. It had changed her.

Had it become love?

Without question, she knew she would do whatever it took to keep Lily safe. She had to reach out to Death and plead for Lily's life, there was no other choice. Doing so would reveal what she felt, and it terrified her. And what about Rowena? She would have to deal with the other Reaper's involvement and threat as well.

Most Reapers were loners, zero attachments. Alex had befriended Rowena when she was her apprentice. They had become more than Reaper and apprentice. Their relationship wasn't unique for her kind but there weren't many who consummated those relationships.

Alex's mistake was never seeing Rowena for what she was. A power-hungry bitch with an ultimate goal, to usurp Alexandra Dante's role within the Reaper hierarchy.

She didn't doubt that Rowena had feelings for her but that night twenty years before had revealed the bitter truth. Rowena was out for Rowena.

Alex knew that Death had a fondness for her. She had never understood why, but she had worked hard for her status. She was willing to trade it all for Lily's life.

She smiled as the woman in question threw her leg over Alex's. She tried to stay still, but she must have tensed in some way.

"Alex?" A sleepy Lily rolled onto her back. "What's wrong?"

"Nothing's wrong, everything is perfect." Alex opened her arms and let Lily spoon into her. Holding her felt right. "Go back to sleep, it's still early."

Lily purred as she snuggled in. "'Kay..."

Hot water coursed down Lily's back easing the soreness she felt after last night's events. No one had ever made love to her the way Alex had. It scared her. She was feeling things for this woman, this Reaper, that she had never felt for anyone.

Alex was gone when she woke up. The simple note she'd left on her pillow had tempered any feelings of abandonment Lily had felt.

Be back shortly, had to take care of something. Would rather be with you.

Alex

She couldn't stop the memories and feelings from the previous night from washing over her. This was by far the craziest thing she had ever done and she had done a lot of crazy things.

But even with her feelings threatening to rule her decisions, she knew enough to keep her head. She shouldn't be here. This world was a complete unknown to her and besides, what did she really know about Alex?

The fact that she called herself a Reaper should terrify her and yet ever since they shook hands a few days ago, she had felt connected to her in a way that was definitely unnatural but right.

Lily hesitated over the scar. It was a part of her life, a part of who she was and somehow it connected her to Alex. She needed answers. The groundswell of emotion she felt for the other woman threatened to overwhelm her. It was on a level she wasn't familiar with at all.

Giving in to her baser needs last night had been a mistake and quite unlike her.

But you loved every minute didn't you Lil?

With the water growing cold she finally stepped out and wrapped one of the oversized towels around herself. She just wanted to get dressed and try to figure out how to get out this damned hotel room.

She stopped in the middle of the room and looked around in shock. Her clothes were missing.

The only clothes she had, were what she had worn yesterday, and now those clothes were gone.

It was obvious someone had been in the room. The bed had been made, the pillows on the couch had been straightened and there was a covered meal tray on the table.

"Are you flipping kidding me?" She stomped over to the closet and yanked the door open. What had to be Alex's duffle lay on the floor. Resigning herself to wearing clothes that were not her own, she opened it up and started rummaging around, pulling out a pair of jeans.

With no underwear in sight, she just put them on.

"Commando it is." She muttered. She was forced to roll up the pants given that Alex was several inches taller than her.

Grabbing the shirt she had worn as a nightshirt, she put that on as well, grateful that she wasn't as well-endowed as some of her friends since her bra was one of the items now missing.

Drying her hair as best she could she looked in vain for a comb or brush. Resigned, she used her fingers to comb through the loose tangles and tried to ignore the rumbling in her stomach.

The tempting aroma emanating from the covered meal tray finally drew her to it. Angry as she was at being left locked in, alone, and basically naked, she couldn't fight how ravenous she felt.

Expectations high, she took a bite. The light fluffy eggs

practically melted in her mouth and the sausages held a hint of maple. Lily smiled as she dabbed at her lips. She had definitely burned a lot of calories last night.

With her hunger abated, she examined her options.

She could just sit back and wait for Alex to come back and demand to go home, or she could try to figure a way out.

Lily got up and eyed the door, decision made. When she pulled on the door, she was surprised to find it unlocked. It made her pause. Alex had obviously wanted her to stay put for a reason, but her curiosity got the better of her. Jamming her feet into her shoes she stepped out making sure she grabbed her bag on the way.

Without the distraction of Alex beside her, she could appreciate just how impressive the hallway she had walked through twice actually was. It was as opulent as the lobby she had seen the day before.

The lush carpet was a deep blood red and the gold trim around the lights gave the hallway a certain glow. She headed toward the sounds of conversation and hoped that Alex wouldn't be to mad at her.

Chapter
Fourteen

By the time she made it to the front desk, Lily had been sniffed at, poked and invited to do some unspeakable things she didn't know were possible.

Finding no one at the desk she turned to make sure nothing or no one got to close.

She jumped when someone tapped her on the shoulder.

"Are you okay miss?" The clerk she'd been introduced to the day before was looking at her with concern.

"No dammit I'm not okay. What is this place and where the hell is Alex?!"

She knew she was yelling, but she didn't care. She wanted to go home. The wonderful night she'd had was quickly fading into memory.

"There she is."

Lily whipped her head around at the whispered words. The pale group of two women and one man were practically eating her with their eyes.

"What the hell are you looking at?" She swallowed nervously when they just laughed and walked away.

She cursed when Ava tapped her again, having forgotten the other woman was even there.

"Miss, maybe you should go back to your room."

"It's not my room, it's Alex's. My room is in San Francisco and I don't think I'm anywhere near that right now."

When a shifter got to close, Ava intervened. "Miss…"

"Please stop calling me that, my name is Lily." She kept a wary eye on the misshapen thing that kept licking its fingers as it watched her.

She didn't know how long she stood there before the thing finally slunk away. Letting out a sigh of relief she turned to see the clerk eyeing her with concern.

"Miss Lily can I at least escort you to the bar? You can wait for Ms Alex there."

And you won't be so obvious. She didn't say the words aloud, but Lily knew what she was thinking.

"Sure…look, I'm sorry I'm a little-"

"No worries miss. I would think Ms Alex doesn't want anything to happen to you." Her grin did nothing to appease the growing anxiety causing a knot in Lily's stomach.

LILY SAT at a corner table while Ava went to find Selena. She didn't really want to speak to the woman, but Ava seemed convinced that Selena would help her feel better. She doubted it.

She pulled Alex's shirt tight around her as she tried to disappear in the seat. Soft music was playing, and she was thankful the bar was almost empty, there was no one else she had to deal with. She let her mind drift thinking about Alex and where she could possibly be.

Lily woke with a start when the music stopped, surprised that she had fallen asleep. She wasn't alone.

"Selena?!" The woman's eyes were unnerving and missed nothing.

"I'm surprised to see you here." Her voice was soft and much gentler than the last time she'd heard it.

Lily ran a finger along her shirt collar and wondered what to say. She didn't want to offend anyone but it was obvious that nothing was what it seemed, even someone as normal looking as Selena.

Selena followed Lily's hand as it traced the outline of her scar knowing full well that with the connection the women had, it wouldn't be long before Alex turned up.

"I was a bit conspicuous at the front desk. I think Ava figured I wouldn't create as much of a ruckus in here."

Selena smiled. The woman was definitely strong willed, trying to maintain a semblance of normalcy after being placed in a strange situation.

"Well, given that Alex should be along soon, I see no problem with you staying here. Would you like something to drink?"

Confused, Lily tried to process what she said. "How do you know when she will be back?"

Selena inclined her head, "Your scar, you're connected you know." She got up and walked back to the bar.

"Hey! Wait a minute!" Indignation replaced anxiety. When she grabbed the other woman by the arm, she knew she'd made a big mistake.

Selena grabbed her hand and turned, eyes flashing green.

Lily winced at the strength in the woman's grip, but she refused to cower.

"Don't touch me." The bartender released her hand and kept walking.

"Please, I didn't mean to grab you, but what did you mean when you said we're connected?"

Selena paused for a moment before finally turning to face her.

"She hasn't told you." It was a statement not a question.

"She...Alex?" Lily shook her head, "I don't understand."

Selena tried to quell her growing frustration with the Reaper. It was not her place to say anything to this woman and yet here she was.

"You can wait here for Alex. I assure you, no one will bother you."

"But-"

"No, it is not for me to say. Alex will be along shortly, I suggest you two...talk."

CHAPTER
FIFTEEN

Alex shifted from one foot to the other. The room she was waiting in was austere and cold. The lackluster decorating didn't match its owner. Contrary to what he stood for, Death was flamboyant, not austere at all.

She had been ready to seek an audience with him but instead, Death had summoned her to his home before Lily had woken up, and she was more than a bit nervous. She knew it had to have something to do with either Lily or Rowena or both.

She thought back to when she and Rowena had been friends. Rowena had always been pushy and she had wanted more than just friendship. There were feelings between them that had been left unresolved after the events twenty years ago, feelings that she should have faced. Instead, that night had resulted in both women being elevated within the Reaper ranks, each going their separate ways.

They should have been satisfied with how things had turned out after that night, but that had never been the case. It pissed her off that it had come to this.

Her thoughts were interrupted by one of Death's personal guard. The woman was nondescript, gray even and her voice was like a hushed whisper as she ushered Alex in to meet with him.

"Alexandra!" The tall gentleman spoke with a hint of a European accent and presented himself in the traditional garb of an eighteenth-century European aristocrat. He was the only one to always call her by her full name.

He extended a hand which she took dutifully, kissing the large ring he wore. The effect of the ring was immediate. Her limbs suddenly felt heavy and her breath, labored. The charge she had gotten from spending the night with Lily was stripped away.

"Hmm...delicious." Death licked his fingers. "How extraordinary. How did you do it?"

"Sir?" Alex shook her head feeling drained. Death forced everyone in his presence to kiss that damned ring. Insurance he called it.

"The human, I could taste it." He waved a hand at the sofa in the room. "Sit, sit. We have some business to sort through." He took a seat in one of the large chairs that bore a striking resemblance to a throne.

Alex settled in and kept a wary eye on him. He was in too good a mood and it scared her.

"Alexandra...you seem a bit nervous."

He knew. He knew about Lily.

"Sir..." The word caught in her throat when he smiled at her.

"Relax Alexandra, we're just going to have a little talk." He took a drink from a large goblet on the side table and dabbed at both sides of his mouth. "Rowena seems rather angry at you. Is there something I should know?"

Alex considered her options. There weren't many.

"Not at all. Rowena is always angry at me. Maybe she thinks I slighted her again." She kept her voice as light as possible.

"Now, now...she's a good Reaper." He smiled and gave her a wink. "She had a good teacher though, didn't she?"

"Yes sir, she did. Have you spoken to Basque? He would know better than anyone what Rowena is up to."

"No not yet. I thought I would speak to you first. I haven't seen you in ages Alexandra." His eyes twinkled with mischief.

She didn't trust him for a minute. He loved a good game and he knew a lot more than he was letting on. She knew it in her gut.

"It has been a while sir. I'll definitely try to make it out more often. It's been pretty busy."

"I dare say it has!" He was positively gleeful. "Wars, skirmishes, accidents and of course the usual calls. So many opportunities to advance."

"Yes sir." The sudden pressure in her chest distracted her. *Lily*

"Hmm..." Death responded to her change in tone. "Will you be joining in the upcoming hunt Alexandra?"

Alex blinked away the image of Lily and nodded. "Of course, I wouldn't miss it."

"Good, good. Keep me informed about Rowena. You let me know if she bothers you."

She knew she'd been dismissed and the request to spare Lily she had been determined to make, died on her lips.

DEATH CALLED in another of his personal guard, a small but powerfully built little man.

"Knox, find Basque and bring him here. I have some questions to ask him."

Knox bowed and excused himself. He watched the little man leave and pulled out the note he had received.

It is happening.

He had hoped Alexandra would confide in him, but he hadn't made it easy. He had never seen her as anything but confident. This Alexandra was distracted, weak. Easy prey for someone as ruthless as Rowena.

He ran a finger along some of the old books in his bookcase and pulled out the one he was looking for. Without hesitation, he found the highlighted passage.

They will be marked at death by the harbinger of death
The harbinger will not know peace
The marked one will die at the hand of death
The harbinger will have their release

THE LANGUAGE it was written in was ancient. The rest of the book was a basic love story being played out yet again. This time the main player in the story didn't include him, but the fruit of that first encounter.

Stay on guard Alexandra.

BY THE TIME Alex stepped into the lobby of the hotel she was shaken. Death had to know about Lily, but he had never brought it up. That bothered her more than she cared to admit.

She ignored the greetings and whistles that followed her. It was only when she reached the entrance to the bar that she realized everyone had made a gap for her, seeming to know exactly where she was headed.

"Dammit."

She wasn't surprised to find Lily inside the bar. What did surprise her was who she found her with.

Maddox smiled as he listened to Lily talk about the last climb she'd been on.

"So, you met Alex just a few days ago?"

"Yes, why?"

"Well Alex is a loner you know. She isn't part of a family like we are." He pointed to his brother who was talking to a lovely looking fae with fire red streaks in her hair. "Reapers tend to keep to themselves." The moment he leaned in, Alex had had enough.

"Lily…Maddox…" The words ground out like she was chewing on glass. Maddox took one look into her eyes and swallowed.

"Hey Alex, no foul okay. She was sitting here by herself you know…Selena said it was fine…We kept others away from her you know?" He was stumbling over is words, but Alex heard him.

"Thank you. I owe you." She inclined her head and he gave up his seat but not before saying goodbye.

With a flourish, he took Lily's hand and kissed it. "A pleasure Miss Lily." He winked at Alex as he ran his tongue across lips.

"Damned Weres." Alex cursed under her breath, angry that she let him get to her.

When she finally looked at Lily, she wasn't surprised at the anger flashing in her eyes.

"Lily-"

"You have a lot of nerve. How dare you just leave me like that."

"I can expl-"

"Explain? Oh, I think you have a lot to explain." She pulled open her shirt to expose the scar. "Why are we connected?"

They both ignored the attention they were now getting from everyone.

"Not here." Alex held onto her temper. Lily had every right to be angry but what she was doing right now was dangerous.

"Not here? Not here? Then where Alex? Is that even your name? What the hell is going on?" She was beyond angry and Alex knew it.

She extended her hand but wasn't surprised when Lily ignored it. "Fine. Follow me." She headed to the back-meeting room where she knew Selena would be.

Since Selena had been the one to tell her about the connection, it was time she also told Lily.

CHAPTER SIXTEEN

Selena seemed to know they were coming. She had set out the manuscript Alex had read through and was waiting for them.

Lily took the first seat and refused to look at Alex. Her emotions were all over the place. The moment she'd seen the Reaper her heart had started beating faster and she had to fight the flush that threatened to show how much she remembered about the previous night. She couldn't give her the satisfaction though. Lily had always been in control of her life and now she had none. That didn't sit well with her.

"It seems to me," Selena started, "you two need to talk."

"Selena, I don't-" Alex snapped her mouth shut at Selena's raised hand.

"Alex dear what you think is irrelevant. She deserves to know what is going on. I tried to warn you, but you didn't listen and now you will both have to deal with the consequences." Selena picked up a delicate teacup from the small serving tray Lily hadn't noticed before and sat back.

Lily waited. She saw the struggle in Alex's face and her heart broke a bit at the raw emotion in her eyes.

"Less than five days…"

Alex's mumbled words scared the hell out of her, so she reached out and took Alex's hands in hers.

"Talk to me." Lily's words were frank, but her tone was gentle. When she brought the hands up to her chest, Alex's defenses crumbled.

"I did that to you."

Shocked hands dropped her own as Lily took a step back. "What?"

ALEX FELT LILY'S ANGUISH. How could she not, but she couldn't stop now.

"Twenty years ago, I was there. I took lives on the road that night, it was my job. Families…We were to take families…"

"My parents?" The horror in Lily's voice pained her, but she ignored it.

"There were several of us, shimmering in and out. Touching, calling, taking lives. A fellow Reaper…a fellow Reaper took your parents and tried to take you." She saw a glimmer of understanding dawn in her eyes.

"You stopped them."

Alex nodded. "Barely, I thought you were dead. You were so small and broken. When I saw the gash in your chest, I tried to close it, hold it together, but we were still fighting, she and I, and I left you there. It was Selena who told me you'd survived."

Lily spared Selena a look. "Who is *she*?"

"Rowena Child, she was my apprentice at the time and decided she would make a name for herself that night."

She watched and waited as Lily processed the information she'd given her.

"I still don't understand this...this connection."

Selena finally spoke up.

"When Alex touched you that night, she wasn't taking a life, she was giving it. Something a Reaper hasn't done in recent or even ancient memory. You're linked. Alex was able to ignore it, but when she touched you again..."

"The day of my climb." Lily said.

"Yes, the day of your climb, there was no mistaking it," with a glare toward Alex, Selena continued, "there was also no going back."

Lily turned back to Alex. "How long have you been watching me?"

"You have made it a point to tempt fate at every opportunity..."

"How long Alex?"

"How many times did you get hurt with your death defying stunts? You can't cheat death!"

"HOW LONG!" She said, breast heaving. "Is this why I do all those crazy things? That's what you're saying, isn't it? You say I keep cheating death? Well you did it first!" Lily pushed her away.

Alex stopped her before she got to the door. "Wait! You need to understand."

"Understand what? You're a killer Alex, plain and simple, isn't that what a Reaper is."

Alex felt like she'd been slapped.

"That is quite enough." Selena got up and pulled the manuscript out again. "Sit down, both of you."

"Here." She let Lily read the passage she'd shown Alex.

"She won't be able to read-"

Alex listened as Lily read the words aloud, the ancient language easily understood.

"How?" Alex looked to Selena for answers.

"I told you Alex, connected." Selena got up and headed back out to the bar. "I think you two need to talk a bit more."

When the door shut, Alex looked over at Lily who had continued to read.

"It's a love story." Her voice was filled with wonder.

"What do you mean it's a love story. Selena didn't say anything about that."

Lily pushed the manuscript toward her. "Read for yourself."

Lily paced the room while Alex continued to read. Her hand unconsciously going to her scar. Her life was a lie. A series of unfortunate events. And what about what she felt for Alex, was it even real.

"It is real Lily. What we feel...what I feel is more real than anything I've ever known."

Once again, Alex knew what she was thinking. She let Alex take her by the hand and sat down again.

"Unfortunately, it doesn't stop the fact that in less than five days you become a bounty." Alex's body language reflected the anguish she felt.

"I'm not dead yet." She gave the Reaper a ghost of a smile. "Take me home Alex. If I have only five days, then let me live it on my terms." She thought she understood now how Alex had come to her rescue with Braxton. She was still angry, but not at Alex.

"I won't let them take you Lily." There was no mistaking the desperation in her voice.

"Can you really stop it?"

THE MOMENT they got back to their hotel room Lily started to pace.

"I can't stay here Alex. I need to go home." Lily was exasperated. Alex was being intransigent, but it had been two of the most wonderful days of her life thus far.

They argued, they yelled, they loved, but in the end, Alex acquiesced and brought Lily back to the little building by the river where they had first entered the Hotel. The sun was just beginning to set.

"I need you to let me go" Lily fought the tears that threatened to fall again. She'd never been in love and all she wanted to do was hang on to Alex, but she knew that was the wrong thing to do. She had her own life to live no matter how much time she had.

"I can't"

Standing outside her car, Lily saw the look in Alex's eyes and knew she was serious.

"Alex I-"

"No! I will not say goodbye to you Lily. I asked you once to trust me, do it now. I will figure this out." She grabbed Lily's hand and placed it where her own heart would be. "You gave me something and now I need to give it back."

Lily fully expected the kiss, but it still took her breath away. There was a promise in it and Lily believed her.

Alex held onto her as long as she was allowed but Lily finally pushed her away and got into her car.

It seemed like forever since she'd been in it and as she drove away, she caught a glimpse of Alex's duster blowing in the wind before she shimmered away.

When Lily finally let herself into her apartment a half hour later, she felt like she was visiting a complete stranger's apartment. Her things were there and it was her home of course but it felt barren, empty. Had she really only been gone just over a day?

An overwhelming urge to see Alex washed over her. Dropping her things by the door she looked for the drawing she had made. The sketch had captured the Reaper's essence and while it was a poor substitute, it would suffice for now.

It wasn't there. She tore up her desk and workspace searching for it as the realization that someone or something had been in her apartment, struck her.

Her harsh laugh as she wiped away a tear mirrored her feelings. It was simple, she wanted Alex with her. Her head was telling her she was crazy and that she'd only known the Reaper for a few days, but in her heart's reality they had already loved a lifetime's worth.

Chapter
SEVENTEEN

Rowena was chomping at the bit. Basque had brought her news of a human with Alex at the Hotel and then had promptly disappeared. That was yesterday.

"Idiot." She was sure he would turn up eventually but in the meanwhile she would cultivate a few more of her sources and find out just what happened between Alex and her little human.

"Did you just call me an idiot?" There was no mistaking the growl in Maddox' voice.

"No of course not." She poured him another drink. "So, tell me more about this human."

Rowena sat back and listened as Maddox talked about the altercation he and his brother had with Alex and the human she had been so protective of just two days ago. She knew now that Alex had at the very least spent a night with the woman if not two. They had left the Hotel and there weren't many willing to talk to her about them.

When Selena came by to ask her if she wanted another drink she replied with a tight smile.

"No, thank you. Maddox here might though."

"Damn straight!" His drunken voice rose. "I got a Reaper sitting with me!"

Rowena shook her head. He *was* an idiot. She watched as Selena poured him a drink and stayed just within earshot.

She didn't care. In less than four days Rowena would have her prize and there was nothing Alex could do about it. She pulled the drawing out of her pocket and cursed when it was snatched out of her hand.

"Hey, that's Alex." His wolf whistle raised her hackles. "She's looking hot in that picture."

"Give it back Maddox." She kept her voice controlled but her rage was threatening to explode out of her.

"Relax Rowena, I'll give it back." He turned it over in his hand. "Where'd you get it?"

Her voice changed and he froze. "I said give...it...back."

He paled as his hand shook and the sketch fell out of his hand.

"Rowena!"

Rowena released him and glared at the woman who'd yelled at her. "Stay out of this Selena."

"Do you want to be banned from the Hotel? If you do, go right ahead I'm sure only his brother will miss him." They stared each other down for several minutes before Rowena looked away. Damn that woman. She watched as a shaken Maddox was half carried out of the bar by his brother. Without a word, she picked up the sketch he had dropped and smoothed it out before folding it neatly and putting it back in her pocket.

"I'm sure you want me to leave now right?" She snarled at the bartender as she brushed past her. There was no love lost between them especially since the woman had a known soft spot for Alex.

She looked toward the fountain and imagined what had happened when Maddox and Jax had sniffed around Lily Heatherton. Alex had always been all fire and brimstone. She missed that.

"Rowena!"

Basque jogged up to her from the front desk ignoring the comments from those in the lobby.

"Where the hell have you been?" His appearance snapped her back to the present.

"You're not gonna believe it. Death summoned me."

She stiffened knowing full well it had to something to do with the upcoming hunt.

"Not here." She hissed. "Come on." They couldn't discuss anything here, too many eyes and ears. Besides, she wanted to keep tabs on Alex's pet.

"Where are we going?"

"Where do you think?"

Lily paddled as fast as she could, using her paddle now and then as a rudder. This impromptu little whitewater trip was exactly what she needed and she was grateful for her agent's insistence on getting more water shots.

Her agent wanted water shots; Lily would get more water shots.

There were of course other things she could be taking care of in these last few days, but this was a bit of pleasure she wanted for herself.

She was quite aware of the clock ticking down and for the past two days she had quietly been taking care of handling her affairs. She had even freaked out her friend Roz when she had offered the woman her condo if anything ever happened to her.

She knew Roz was chalking it up to what had happened with Braxton and she hadn't corrected her. Other things she had put in place had been to set up a trust so that the proceeds of her work would go directly to the only family she had left. Her cousin on her mother's side lived in Virginia and was raising her two little girls by herself. The trust would go a long way in helping her stay solvent.

Thinking about it, she truly had been busy, forwarding her prints, cataloging her work, including some works in progress that she would likely never get to. Still, her biggest regret right now was not finding the sketch of Alex.

She had rebuffed all of Alex's attempts to talk with her over the past two days. It felt like a piece of her died inside her each time she did so, but she felt the need to distance herself, from everyone.

Her only fear was that Alex wouldn't answer when she did finally call.

Working the current she let the spray of water hitting her wash away her worries at least for a little while.

For the first time since the death of her parents, Lily felt free.

"Hey, she's pretty good, isn't she?"

Rowena ignored Basque's commentary and watched as Lily fought a dangerous part of the rapids that threatened to overturn her. When the woman righted herself, Rowena could only curse under her breath.

This woman truly did have nine lives.

After talking with Basque about his conversation with Death, she had been hard pressed not to throttle him. He had apparently told Death everything they had been looking into and now he was looking at the records himself.

"Idiot."

"What?" Basque turned on her. "What was that?"

"Nothing Basque. Did he give you any insight on what he was thinking after you spoke to him?"

"He? Oh, the boss? No... no....he just seemed really interested in your falling out with Alex. Really focused you know? It was kind of hard to concentrate...sorry."

She knew he was sorry. Kissing Death's ring made even something as simple as remembering a chore. Only the strong willed and strong minded could fully remember their encounters with him.

They waited a full two days to see if he would summon Rowena, but he hadn't, and that fact had made her furious when Basque told her Alex had been to see Death as well.

Furious was an understatement. The more time passed, the more intense her feelings. She didn't understand what was happening to her, but she knew it was tied to Alex and that girl. Reapers didn't normally experience feelings the same way other creatures did. When they did, they were usually more pronounced and it bothered her to have no control over their intensity.

Rowena smiled. She would use those feelings though and the instincts that had gotten her this far to finally get back at Alex for casting her aside.

"You all right?"

"Hmm? Oh yes." She watched with a keen eye as Lily went around a dangerous curve. With a hint of a smile she shimmered away just ahead of Lily and made sure the tree that had come down in the last storm just happened to break free from the shore.

"Such an unfortunate accident."

CHAPTER EIGHTEEN

Lily held her breath as she took the sharp curve and had just a moment to realize the danger. The tree branch caught her across the chest, knocking the wind out of her and rolling the kayak.

With a large part of the tree under water, she found herself caught against its trunk. The rushing water slamming into her as she struggled to right herself. Black motes filled her eyes as the lack of oxygen threatened to overwhelm her.

She was panicking. She couldn't get the kayak unstuck so her only option was to get out of it. The cold water slowed her fingers as she undid the skirt holding her in. Her vest's buoyancy was a godsend because she was out of air and energy as it helped bob her up like a cork next to the kayak.

She took a deep rasping breath and sputtered as the rushing water threatened to submerge her again. Reaching for the hull, she tried to hang on.

An errant rush of water dunked her again and the side of her head slammed into the kayak making her grateful for the helmet she was wearing.

Now what?

The cold water was stealing what energy she had left. She had to either get out of the water or back in the kayak. Taking a deep breath, she forced herself under to see if she could find where the kayak was caught.

It took her four tries and another two to work it free and figure out how to use the tree to help her. By the time she got back into the kayak her teeth were chattering so hard she couldn't hear herself think. One thing was certain, she needed to get to her campsite.

Her paddle was gone. An experienced kayaker, she pulled out the smaller emergency paddle strapped to the inside of the kayak and notched the two halves together. It was now or never.

Once she pulled away there was still the chance that another part of the tree would catch her again but she was betting that she could use the current to steer her way clear of it.

Lily waited for a few minutes and caught a heavy rush of water out into the middle of the river just managing to clear the tree.

It hurt to breathe. She figured she had at least a bruised rib or two thanks to that branch and a doozy of a headache, but she was alive.

"Take that Reapers."

BASQUE KEPT his mouth shut while Rowena tore apart a deer. Her rage was frightening. When she shimmered away he hadn't known what to think, but hearing her laughing along the shore had made him curious.

He watched as the human that two Reapers were fixated

on, struggled to stay alive.

He had to admit, he was impressed with the human's resilience. Another person might have given up. When Rowena moved forward to insure the woman stayed under, Basque had grabbed her.

Their argument had been brief and vicious. The bruise on his face clear evidence of her rage.

He waited. When she was finally done, she looked like images that people had painted of Reapers, her true face shimmered in and out as she tried to control herself and the blood dripping from her hands matched the venom that dripped from her words.

"How dare- "

"I dare." He shook his head at her. "Of course, I dare! She's marked, what the hell are you thinking?" He screamed. "You can't take her without- "

"Without...without what? Permission?" She pushed him away from her and sat on a fallen tree. "We had permission, twenty years ago."

Basque didn't know what else to say to her. She was out of control and for a Reaper, that was beyond dangerous.

They took a life when it was time and for a bounty. That was it. Not this...

"Rowena," his voice was as soothing as he could make it, "it's just a couple more days. You know how to track her, you have the advantage."

"Do I Basque?"

He didn't know how to answer her.

***

ALEX BREATHED a sigh of relief when she saw Lily's head bobbing in the water. She had to fight every instinct she had to try and help her, but she held back, knowing full well her interference would not be appreciated.

She winced and had to fight the unnatural instinct to go to her, when Lily struck her head. She could almost feel Lily's physical pain.

Lily had asked Alex to let her go but she couldn't and wouldn't. She had read through the story that prophesied this connection between them and the clearest information she had been able to find was that this had happened before.

Selena had tried to dissuade her of that, but the more she read, the more she realized that the story wasn't a story at all. It was a journal, and if she could find out who wrote it, she might be able to figure out how to save Lily.

In less than two days, Reapers would be out hunting for this one human. Alex had spoken to a few of them and had traded some favors and bounties for them to look the other way. Some had taken her up on the offer knowing that Alex's bounties were generally ones of notice. Others had laughed in her face.

There was one option she had considered, but not followed through on when she had the chance, to plead for Lily's life directly to Death. She didn't even know if it was possible to do so, besides, he was angry that Lily had been so adept at cheating him for the past twenty years.

But then that was her fault.

She may well be able to leverage that fact and save Lily's life, but an act like that would have consequences...for her.

Lost in thought she was surprised when Lily's kayak passed by her in the water. Seeing her filled Alex with a warmth that was still foreign to her but she understood it now. Love.

The old man was right

She shimmered away with a smile.

A‍lex continued watching her, this time not far from where she was to camp, as she navigated her way down the rapids. It was a thing of beauty to watch her in action.

Breast heaving, the sinews in Lily's arms stood out against her skin. They weren't overly defined, but Alex knew from personal experience just how strong they were as Lily held the paddle controlling her route down the river.

It was abhorrent to her that Lily went on these trips by herself. She was tempting fate, especially after what had just happened. But she understood why.

Understanding wasn't enough though and she sincerely hoped Lily was ready to hear her out.

CHAPTER NINETEEN

Lily rinsed off the cuts on her arms and head before hazarding a look at her ribcage. Hesitant, she lifted the shirt. A nasty bruise was already making its appearance and she winced as she felt around it.

"Dammit!" She could tell she had cracked at least one if not two ribs. Tears of frustration gathered in her eyes. Her plan had been to spend the night and then head down to the pick-up site but she was beat.

Bad enough she only had a couple of days before Death came after her, but to spend them hurt just aggravated her.

"Ugh..."

"Lily..."

"Son of a..." Lily winced as the sudden movement jarred her ribs. "Dammit Alex, will you please stop popping in and out like that, it freaks me out."

"I'm sorry." She saw Lily holding a hand to her ribs and frowned.

"I know I told you I would leave you alone for a couple days, but we need to talk."

Lily saw shadows under Alex's eyes that matched her own. "I can't- "

"Lily please." Pleading, Alex grabbed her hands. The jolt both felt was shocking.

Lily impulsively brought Alex's hand up to the scar on her chest and was stunned at the heat that flowed through her. She didn't know how long they stood like that before she collapsed to the ground.

"Lily!" Alex dropped down next to her, worry colored her raspy voice.

She could breathe easily again. Lifting her shirt, she looked at the bruise across her midsection. Instead of a fresh injury, it looked like it was days old and instead of the sharp pain of just a few moments ago, it was a dull ache.

"How?"

Alex shook her head looking down at her hands. She felt drained but content.

"I'm not sure."

"Is that what you did the other night when Braxton attacked me? And the night of the accident?" Lily's voice shook. "Is that how you marked me?"

"I...I'm not sure."

Lily let Alex help her up, wanting nothing more than to know the answer but it didn't look like Alex had a clue.

"It's okay. Weird things appear to be the norm for me anymore." She grabbed her pack and started pulling stuff out to set up camp.

When she didn't get a response, she turned to face the Reaper only to find her staring.

"What?"

"We need to talk."

Alex waited until the woman she loved, took a seat.

"I need you to come back to the Hotel with me." As the request spilled out she braced herself for Lily's response.

"Alex..."

"Hear me out, please." When Lily nodded, she continued.

Alex paced. She wanted this woman safe and with her, but she was so strong willed and independent she knew Lily had to do things on her terms. She knew some of the personal things Lily had taken care of since hearing of the bounty and that she was prepared to meet Death, but there was still a chance.

"I'm going to speak to Death and ask for your life."

Lily started to object.

"I need you to come back and go through the manuscript with me. See what I don't see. In the meantime, I know you'll be safe and I can go speak to him on your behalf. I can explain that this is all a misunderstanding. That it was all my fault. You shouldn't have to pay the price for what I did."

Lily wrapped her arms around the Reaper and just held on.

Surprised, Alex had no words, so she did the only thing she could, she held onto her for dear life.

"I can't let you do that Alex." Lily shook her head. "Won't he want something from you? From us?"

Alex sat her down. "Possibly...no, likely, but there's more."

Alex told her about the paintings and pictures where Lily had captured Death and she saw understanding in her eyes.

"So, it's not just what happened twenty years ago?"

"I think everything is linked. I believe the only reason that you can photograph those things is your connection to me."

"But then how do we resolve that without...oh..."

Alex let the bitterness spill from her. "We have to find a way to break the bond."

CHAPTER TWENTY

It took some doing but she was finally able to convince Lily that going back to the Hotel was the way to go.

Lily was not happy with this turn of events and told her so. The idea of breaking a bond that she'd had for the past twenty years however unknowingly, was painful.

Decision made they decided to go back to Lily's condo the traditional way, like humans. Reaper and woman both, loaded up the kayak and trekked through the woods to Lily's car.

Lily couldn't hold back her mirth whenever Alex tripped over a tree root.

"You don't do this much, do you?" She teased.

"No...I don't." Alex pulled on her duster when it caught on one of the bushes. Mournful, she begged her lover. "Can't we just- "

"Absolutely not!" Lily stifled an absurd giggle when she heard Alex mutter something under her breath. "Was that French?"

"Oui." Alex loved the smile that crossed her face.

"Hmm...sexy."

This time when Alex tripped, Lily did laugh out loud.

By the time they made it back to her place it was getting dark. While Lily put away her gear and packed an overnight bag, Alex took that time to look at who Lily had become as a woman.

The family picture of Lily and her parents was proudly displayed on the table by the window. She wasn't surprised to see that it was taken shortly before the accident. Lily looked exactly as she did on the night Alex had first seen her.

She thought back to the overwhelming grief she had felt from Lily when they first touched after her climb and wished she could truly understand. She could feel it, but she could never understand it.

She shook herself and looked around. There were several large prints of Lily's pictures in a corner and as she rifled through them, she wasn't surprised to find at least one that had raised the alarm for Reapers and helped to put a target on Lily's back.

It baffled her how Lily could capture those images. Rubbing her fingers together she wondered if she played a part in that as well.

She knew a lot about Lily but not the personal things, the intimate things and she wondered if they would ever have a chance to explore them.

The last two days for her had been spent researching and exploring the new emotions that had revealed themselves. Unfortunately, without Lily's presence she didn't know what to do or how to feel. The manuscript hadn't revealed much more than what she had already found and she refused to accept that Lily had to die.

She picked up a picture of Lily taken after one of her climbs. The smile on her face was full of life. She had a cut on her face and her jacket was torn, but there was a look of pure satisfaction. Alex remembered that climb. She had almost made her presence known then. The rockslide that Lily and her fellow climbers had been caught in had almost cost the group of them their lives. There were several Reapers present that day, Alex included but her goal was a singular one. Keep Lily alive.

Fate had stepped in and provided the group with some cover. The injuries were minor for the most part, but it had been a scary feeling for Alex. The other Reapers had been disgusted and left. Alex had stayed and she remembered watching Lily pose for the picture.

That had been three years ago. She felt more for her today. Much more.

Lily stood in the hallway as Alex roamed her living room. It surprised her to see the sadness in the Reaper's body language, and she wondered if Alex felt like she did. If she could feel that way.

Besides almost drowning, the most shocking thing for her today, was the emotion that had filled her when Alex had popped in on her by the river. Her presence had immediately filled an emptiness Lily hadn't realized existed. She'd missed her. She barely knew her, but she had missed her.

That's when it hit her.

Love. This is what love felt like. This is what her parents had for each other. This is what she had been searching for her whole life.

Warmth filled her as she thought about the time they had spent together at the Hotel. The feel of the other woman's hand against hers when they had met after her climb. This woman, this Reaper cared for her in a way that no one Lily had ever been with did.

"Alex?"

The Reaper whipped around so quickly Lily took a step back.

"Jesus you're fast."

Alex smiled. "I have to be. Are you ready?"

"Just about." Lily sat on the couch and patted the spot next to her. "Sit, please."

"We should really-"

"Go? Yes, I get it." She patted the couch again. "Humor me. Sit next to me on my couch like all of this is normal."

Alex took a seat. "Lily..."

"Why me?"

She took pity on Alex the moment she said it. She knew Alex blamed herself and her actions twenty years prior.

"Forget it...will you just...hold me?"

"Of course."

Lily leaned into her and let herself enjoy the feel of Alex's arms around her. She could feel Alex's sadness ease along with her own. Come what may. They were good for each other.

CHAPTER
TWENTY-ONE

Lily was more prepared for her entry into the Hotel this time, but she was still struck dumb by the opulence.

The lobby was larger than she remembered but there were also a lot more...people? She could see all manner of different creatures, and the noise. There were a multitude of languages being spoken, only a few of which she recognized.

She stopped in her tracks when a beautiful blonde walked up to Alex and kissed her on the lips before walking out the door they had come through.

Alex for her part seemed shocked and embarrassed by the overt display of affection.

"Someone you know?" Lily couldn't keep the edge out of her voice.

Alex rubbed her mouth with the back of her hand.

"You could say that. She contracted for a death that I took care of."

"What the hell was that, her payment?" Lily tried to keep the jealous tone out of her voice and failed.

Alex grinned at her. "Did that bother you?"

"You know damned well it did."

Alex stopped and pulled her in close. "You have nothing to worry about from her or anyone else." She held her tighter. "You believe me, don't you?"

Lily nodded. Her heart was pounding. The edge of anger and desperation in Alex's voice scared her and she could see it scared Alex as well.

She apologized as she let her go. "I'm sorry Lily, did I hurt you?"

Lily swallowed nervously. What did she really know about this woman, this Reaper? She was trusting her with her life. It was only the things she'd seen at the Hotel that had convinced her of the truth of her situation.

"No...no, you didn't hurt me." She took Alex's hand. "Promise me you won't do that again okay?" Her words held an unmistakable tremor.

Alex sighed. She'd screwed up, again.

"I promise."

"Welcome back Miss Lily." Ava smiled at both women as they approached.

"Thank you. Ava, right?"

"That's correct Miss Lily. Ms Alex here is your key and you have a message again." Her hand trembled as she handed over a note.

Alex reached out mechanically and took the note.

"What was that about?" Lily watched as Ava scurried away. She was surprised when Alex made no move to open the note. "Aren't you going to read it?"

Alex steeled herself for whatever the note might say.

'*History is doomed to repeat itself. E*

Lily craned her neck and read the note. Through body language alone she could tell that Alex was not happy with the note.

"Alex?" Lily moved closer and whispered. "Is it about me?"

Alex sucked in her breath and looked at her, eyes glittering like black onyx. She crumpled the note in her hand and tossed it across the counter.

"No."

Lily didn't believe that for one second, but she could tell that Alex needed it to be true.

ALEX COULD SENSE Lily's anxiety as they walked through the lobby. The beings in the lobby hadn't made it easy as taunts and praise were both thrown their way. Only Lily's hold on her arm had stopped her from ramming those taunts down some throats. One comment had sent a shiver down her spine.

Go let Rowena know she's back.

It didn't surprise her that Rowena had asked to be notified, it bothered her though to know how many in the lobby seemed to have a bloodlust about it. She felt Lily shift in her arms as she shoved off the hand of a being who'd touched her.

"Come on." She pulled Lily away and headed to their room. There was more going on and she wondered what Rowena had said about this particular bounty.

ALEX OPENED the door to her room and breathed a sigh of relief as Lily placed her bag on the bed and looked back at her.

"That was interesting," her voice dripped with sarcasm. "So, what now?"

"Well…I actually need to go to work for a little while. Do you mind staying here by-"

"Absolutely not. You brought me here and now you're going to leave me again? And after all that nonsense in the lobby? No. Let me go with you."

Alex froze. Go with her? "You can't…I mean I can't take you with me."

"Why not?" Lily sat on the bed. "Is it dangerous?"

"No, not this one."

"Then take me with you." Her tone was serious. "I need to know what to expect. You know, what to prepare for."

"Lily you are not-"

"Going to die?" She got up and stood toe to toe with her. "We both know I very likely am. I've tempted death for longer than most are allowed to. Can you at least let me see what to expect?"

Alex saw the determination in her eyes and fell in love all over again.

"Fine."

CHAPTER TWENTY-TWO

Lily watched Alex work and couldn't hide the fear she felt as the woman on the bed took her last breath. Is that how easy it was to die?

"This is not easy Lily. Not at all, but it is my job."

Lily would never know if it was the tone of the Reaper's voice or the look she gave her, but in that moment, Lily knew Alex had played a greater part in her parent's death than she had previously stated.

"It *was* you."

"Lily?" Alex didn't recognize her tone.

"No! It was you! You killed my parents!" Her anguished sobs echoed in the small room.

"Shh...Lily, it wasn't like that." She withstood the smaller woman's assault on her before wrapping her up in her arms.

"Lily...Lily, listen to me. It was a job, I told you, nothing else. I stopped when I got to your parents. I stopped!"

Her sobs punctuated the quiet in the room. "Rowena," she sobbed.

"Yes Rowena. I told you, she took that moment, my hesitation, to advance herself." Alex shut her eyes and let her go.

"I thought she had killed you as well. You looked like a broken doll in your parent's mangled car. The jagged piece of metal in your chest..." She shuddered.

Lily watched Alex try to move past the memories of that night. A night she herself could not remember.

"I tried to help you, I did, but I couldn't stop the bleeding and Rowena-"

"Attacked you." Lily's gently spoken words made Alex shudder. "I noticed a scar on your back. Was that her?"

Alex nodded.

"I thought...I thought you all couldn't really hurt each other?" Lily had to know.

The Reaper pulled a small dagger out of her pocket.

"We never know what we may face and obviously not all beings appreciate our presence."

The heaviness in her heart lifted a bit when she gazed into Alex's eyes.

"Yes but-"

"I don't think Rowena was thinking clearly in that moment." Alex's voice was gruff and Lily raised an eyebrow as things were suddenly clear.

"Were you involved with her?"

Alex hesitated. Would her answer change things between them? She looked at Lily's tear stained face and knew she deserved the truth.

"Briefly."

Lily bit her lip. She didn't have that much experience with relationships, but she knew enough to know that this was more than personal for Rowena. Reaper or not, betrayal was betrayal.

"That explains it then...you didn't back her then, she

fought back and now you're doubling down on what happened that night by protecting me again."

Alex considered her words. It sounded plausible and certainly helped to explain Rowena's unwavering hatred for Lily. It didn't explain their connection however. That was directly related to the manuscript and her own actions that night. If she was to keep Lily alive, they had to find a way to break the bond.

"I will always protect you." She took Lily's hand and they shimmered away, leaving death behind them if only for a little while.

ALEX TOOK her in her arms the moment they got back to the hotel room.

"Alex-"

Alex smothered her words with a kiss. Lily made a feeble attempt to push away before succumbing to her body's response to Alex. This time there was no exploring, it was pure conquest.

By the time they fell onto the bed, they had knocked a lamp over and neither woman had a shirt on.

Lily gasped when Alex's tongue traced around her scar and settled on her breast. Her back arching in response to the nipping and tugging as her nails raked across Alex's back in response.

Alex grunted at the twinge of pain her nails caused. The pounding between her legs was matched by the pounding of Lily's heart. An image of a broken Lily flashed in her head and she hesitated, pulling back, but Lily's response was immediate and she pulled her back down.

There was an urgency in their frenzied lovemaking. Both

were aware of their limited time and both were determined to feel as much as they could in the time they had. By the time they were replete, they had taken each other to the edge and over multiple times.

Hours later, laying side by side, they relished the feel of each other's skin as they lay naked on Alex's bed. Alex rolled over and started trailing kisses down her abdomen stopping at a scar along Lily's hip.

"I was there you know...The day this happened." Her rough voice was full of emotion.

"What...what do you mean you were there?" She caught her breath when Alex gently nipped at the scar.

"The day you fell. You came close to dying that day again."

Lily remembered the incident vividly. A little over a year ago, she had missed a rock outcropping on a climb and fallen almost 30 feet. The ledge she landed on had broken her fall and her pelvic bone.

Alex's lips continued their journey and when she captured a breast, Lily had to stop herself from crying out. If she were to die right now she would be happy.

"Why...oh..."

She shuddered as Alex suckled her breast and gently pushed her away.

"Why didn't you ever show yourself to me?"

Alex looked her in the eye. "I wanted to...I should have...but I thought we had time."

Strong hands pinned Lily to the bed. This was a side of Alex she hadn't seen before. She was talking as if this may well be one of their last times together.

"I love you Lily." Alex froze as the words spilled out of her.

Lily's heart jumped erratically and she grabbed Alex by the back of the head, pulling her down to share a kiss.

"I love you too." Her breathless words were all the permission Alex needed to take her again.

CHAPTER
TWENTY-THREE

Alex looked up at the ceiling and cursed softly as the light of a new day dawned in the room. One day. There was one full day left before the Reapers would be free to go after Lily. The woman in question slept soundly by her side. Rolling over she thought about their options. There weren't many. There was no way she could fight off the Reapers that went after Lily and even the Hotel wouldn't be able to keep her safe.

But she did feel safe here, they both did. Ava had sent up a meal for them that they'd enjoyed in between their night of love making. She smiled, wondering how Ava had known to time room service to get there in between their trysts.

She felt whole, complete with Lily by her side. And she had to admit, she felt stronger than she ever had. She wondered if that had something to do with their connection or their lovemaking. Either way she knew she had to go back to her original decision.

She would go to Death and make her plea. It was all she could think to do. Surely Death would hear her out?

The words from the manuscript played in her head like a broken record.

> *They will be marked at death by the harbinger of death.*
> *The harbinger will not know peace*
> *The marked one will die at the hand of death*
> *The harbinger will have their release*

SHE WAS THE HARBINGER. She was the one who somehow had marked Lily. Was she also the hand of death? Would she somehow be the one to cause her death? She shut her eyes tightly as she thought that through. It hurt. Deep within the recesses of a soul she didn't know she had, it hurt to think of this life, Lily's life, being snuffed out. She would rather give up her own existence if it would save her.

She would wait for Lily to wake, she owed her that, but her decision was made. She would leave Lily behind in the safety of the Hotel to confront Death and offer up a Reaper's life for a human.

WHEN LILY WOKE UP, she reached a hand over to the other side of the bed and found it empty.

"Not again," she groaned.

"Not again what?" Alex walked naked out of the bathroom with just a towel around her waist.

It was rare for Lily to be at a loss for words, but she was.

"Uh...uhm...Dammit you're doing that on purpose."

"Doing what?" Alex threw her a devilish grin as she grabbed her shirt from the edge of the bed.

"You don't play fair you know." Lily sat up and watched as Alex gathered up her things and started getting dressed.

"You're staring love."

Lily blinked back unexpected tears at the endearment. Alex had said that she loved her and she had responded in kind. She had never told anyone she loved them, much less someone like Alex. They were so different and yet so much alike. They had one more day together and as much as she hoped Alex had figured out a way to keep her alive, she had to wonder what it would cost them.

"Have you figured out what you want to do?"

Alex's fingers stopped buttoning her shirt. Hands dropping, she sighed. "I am going to speak to Death. Plead your case. Explain that you had nothing to do with those pictures. That it all goes back to what happened twenty years ago."

"What do you expect him to say?"

"I don't know."

Lily bit her lip as she considered her next words. "What about the journal? Are you going to bring that up?"

Alex took a seat next to her on the bed and held her hand. "I don't know. I'm flying blind here. I'm hoping...damn, I don't know what I'm hoping."

"Can you die?" Lily asked.

If Alex was shocked by her changing the subject, she didn't show it.

"Yes, but not the way humans do."

"What do you mean?"

"It's a little harder to kill us. Death can take my life obviously and there are certain weapons that can hurt me, but all in all we don't die like you do."

"But you *can* die."

"Yes, but Lily-"

"I don't want you to die Alex, not for me."

Alex kissed the back of her hand.

"I don't want you to die either and my goal right now is to keep you alive."

"If it's my time...if I have-"

"No! This is not up for debate. You were spared twenty years ago and there is no reason why that should come back on you now. What happened then was my fault, not yours."

Lily heard her, but it didn't seem to be anyone's fault if you considered the words in the journal.

"I want to go with you."

"To face Death? No, no, no." Alex started pacing the room. "You can't...I mean you're a human."

"You told me he wanted me brought before him, so do it. Bring me to him. Let me plead my own case."

"Lily...

"Please."

CHAPTER
TWENTY-FOUR

Alex held Lily's hand possessively as they walked through the Hotel. She had promised to show Lily more than just the lobby and hotel room before they went to see Death, so they were on their way to one of the ballrooms. The last time Alex had been there had been for a wedding between a Were and a human of all things. It wasn't unheard of, just rare.

Watching Lily walk through the ballroom she could almost imagine her wearing a beautiful gown and holding court on the dance floor. In her mind's eye, she saw herself dressed all in black asking Lily for a dance.

"Alex...Alex!" Lily was watching her with concern. "Where did you go?"

"Nowhere...sorry. Was there anything else you wanted to see?"

"This place is huge, it would take days to see everything and we don't really have that kind of time," she lamented.

"I would love to go back to the bar. I have to admit it

freaked me out a bit when I first went in there, but it grew on me and the things on the wall are fascinating."

Alex could only smile at the excitement in her voice. There was a wonderment that she envied. Both were nervous about what the day would bring but they were determined to face it together.

"Of course. We can speak to Selena and see if she has heard anything."

By the time they made it back to the bar they had been stopped several times.

Most of the beings that stopped them seemed sympathetic, with the only exception being another Reaper they ran into who was definitely in Camp Rowena.

Alex and he had almost come to blows after he described what Rowena wanted to do to Lily before bringing her before Death.

"Everyone knows Alex. There's no winning this one. It's about time someone brought you down a notch." When he punctuated his words by poking her in the chest, Alex reached for her blade. It was Lily who had pulled her back from making a terrible mistake. She'd yanked on her arm before she could respond to him, desperate to pull her away.

"Go on Alex, your pet's calling you."

Alex's growl echoed down the hallway after him.

"Alex, Alex!" Lily held on to her when she tried to follow. "Stop! This is exactly what Rowena wants. Don't let them dictate your actions."

Breast heaving Alex focused on her words. It was fear. Fear of losing Lily that was driving her emotional response and again Lily had kept her centered.

. . .

When they finally went inside the bar the rumor mill was at full blast with just about everyone having heard about the encounter.

They took a booth near the back and were about to call for someone when Selena appeared, drinks in hand.

"How did you know?" Said Alex. She took a sip of the Dragon Whiskey Selena had been gracious enough to pour her, relishing the feel of it coursing through her.

She clicked her tongue. "Now Alex, you know better than that."

"So, what is this?" Lily asked looking at her drink.

"It's a mild drink," Alex said. "Soothing. It will relax you."

Tentative, Lily took a sip from her glass. The clear liquid held just a hint of purple and looked harmless enough. She was wrong.

She sputtered as the spicy drink made its way down her throat. Alex patting her on the back and smiling didn't win her any points.

"I'm fine," she coughed. "I thought you said this was a mild drink?"

"It is," Alex tried to hide the smirk on her face. "Sorry, I'm not trying to laugh at you."

"Oh yes you are." Lily took a chunk of bread from the bowl on the table and stopped short of her mouth, throwing a questioning look at Alex.

"It's just bread Lily."

"That's what you said about the drink." She took a bite and was pleased to feel it absorb some of the spice the drink had left. Ignoring their laughter, she took another bite.

"Thank you, Selena."

"What have you decided?" Selena was speaking to Alex, but Lily knew she was part of the discussion.

"Yes Alex...what *have* you decided?" A silky voice dripping with venom called out from behind them.

"This has nothing to do with you Rowena." Alex's voice was a direct contrast to Rowena's, and they couldn't have been more different.

Lily looked at the woman, or rather, the Reaper, attached to the voice and gave an involuntary shiver. The woman was speaking to Alex but looking directly at her. Coal black eyes pierced her very soul and the hatred in them was lost on no one. If the woman could kill her with a glance, she'd be dead.

Rowena ignored Selena's attempt to block her from sitting and she slid in across from them.

"Oh Alex, of course it has to do with me. Who do you think is going to bring her before Death? I'm claiming her now just as I did twenty years ago."

Alex sprang to her feet. "Get the hell away from her Rowena before I do something I'll regret."

"Will you? Regret it that is..." Rowena smiled knowingly at Alex before touching Lily's hand. "How was your little swim dear?"

Alex launched herself at the other Reaper and started pummeling her. Rowena for her part gave right back. The fight lasted just a few second,s but it was enough for everyone in the bar to take sides. Max's calming and rather large presence separated the two Reapers before any harm had been done.

"Alex..." Selena's warning tone drew her eyes back to Lily. She looked ill and Alex knew it was Rowena's fault.

"We're not done Rowena."

Rowena brushed off her own duster and glared right back at them. "No, but soon." Pushing past the crowd that had gathered she stalked out of the bar leaving Alex to try and help Lily.

"Lily..."

"God..." She coughed. "What did she do to me?" Lily was positively green and grabbing at her midsection.

"Dammit!" Alex lifted Lily's shirt and saw the massive

bruising that had reappeared on her abdomen.

There was no doubt in her mind now that Rowena had been responsible for what happened to Lily on the water yesterday.

"Not here Alex." Selena nodded toward the meeting room. "Take her to the back, it's empty."

Lily's knees buckled as soon as she stood. Alex swept her up in her arms, ignoring the stares and comments from the other patrons she led the way to the back room.

CHAPTER
TWENTY-FIVE

She laid Lily down on the settee as gently as she could. She knew she could help her, just as she'd done the day before, but she had never done it with an audience before.

With Selena standing over them Alex lay her hand on the scar on Lily's chest. Lily stiffened as Alex's hand grew hot before mercifully passing out. Selena caught Alex as she wobbled.

"Is she okay?" Alex sat down next to her, ignoring the trembling of her hands.

Selena didn't say anything for a moment as she realized what she had witnessed. The connection between them was stronger than she had been given to believe.

"She is. How are you?"

Alex leaned forward. "Tired."

Selena left the room and came back with the bottle of Dragon Whiskey.

"Drink, it will help."

Alex didn't question her. She took a swig and let the

warmth course through her. She felt better and she wondered again about its properties but that was something for another day. Rowena was out for blood. Lily's blood. She had to speak to Death before the dawn or there would be no going back.

"I need to speak to Death. I need to plead her case and mine." Alex spoke absently unaware that Lily had opened her eyes.

"*We* need to speak to him," she whispered.

"Lily!" She turned and helped her sit up. "Are you okay?"

Lily nodded and shook out her hand.

"What's wrong?"

"My hand, it's tingling where Rowena touched it. Alex...she made me feel dirty." Alex could tell the admission bothered her.

"What the hell was that about Selena?"

Selena paced the room her long skirt trailing behind her.

"I agree with you. You need to go see him and you need to take her with you." She cursed in a language Alex wasn't familiar with. "He knows about the manuscript."

"What the hell do you mean?" Alex's voice shifted and Lily gasped as she caught a glimpse of her face.

"Alexandra watch your tone!" Selena saw the look of shock on Lily's face.

"Merde!" Alex kneeled in front of Lily and took both of her hands. "Lily...Lily look at me."

Eyes squeezed tight Lily refused. The face she saw wasn't the person she fell in love with.

"Lily please...it's me..."

Whether it was Alex's plea or the overwhelming love she felt for her, Lily finally opened her eyes.

"What...what did I see Alex? And don't lie to me please." It was Lily's turn to plead.

"I'm a Reaper Lily. I am tied to Death and there are times...

there are times when the other side of me is exposed." Alex brought Lily's hands up to her face. "This is me though. I'm still the same person you met a few days ago. I love you Lily, please try to understand."

Lily focused on her eyes. They were the same eyes. Tentative, she ran her fingers over Alex's face, following the contours and high cheek bones. It was still her.

"You realize that scared the hell out of me. You know that, right?"

"I do and I'm sorry. I should have told you."

"Yes, well we haven't exactly had much of a chance to get to know one another that way. Or at least I don't know that much about you." She didn't mean to admonish but when Alex put her head down, Lily made her look at her. "I'm not blaming, just stating."

"I know. It doesn't make it any less true."

"We don't have much time Alex."

No," Selena said. "You don't."

***

Death's private guard were not inclined to let a human in. It took Alex quite some time to convince them that there was no ulterior motive. It wasn't until she mentioned the hunt set for the harvest moon that they acquiesced to letting her in with Lily.

"I thought that would be easier." Lily said.

"So did I." They had taken their time getting their bearings after the run in with Rowena. Selena had gotten them both some food and they had taken the time to read through the manuscript again.

It was obvious that the journal told the tale of a similar incident that had occurred a long time ago. But there were gaps. Gaps in the journal that didn't really speak to survival except for a child. The result of the union, the love story had resulted in the birth of a child, but the entries ended abruptly.

"What do you think happened to the child?" Lily was fascinated with the story even though it seemed to foretell her own death. The idea of a child, a love child she called it, surviving, fascinated her.

"I don't know and right now, I don't care." Alex pulled her close. "You on the other hand, I care about."

Lily looked down at her watch. It was almost ten p.m. If she went by Alex's reckoning, at midnight or a bit thereafter she was free game. A shiver ran through her. She was scared. Not scared of dying per se. She was scared for Alex. Alex was here to bargain for her life and she didn't know what that could cost her.

"Alex...I want you to let me talk to him."

"We talked about this already. Absolutely not." She saw her face and continued. "I'm sure he will ask you questions but please don't address him unless he speaks to you and I need you to promise me you will let me say what I've come to say."

She was about to object when the large doors at the far end of the room opened.

CHAPTER TWENTY-SIX

Alex let herself feel hopeful when Death walked into the room, but that hope was dashed when she saw Rowena walk in behind him. She felt Lily squeeze her hand and she responded hoping to reassure her.

"Alexandra my dear. What are you doing here so late?" He didn't spare Lily a glance, keeping his focus on the Reaper before him. When he extended his hand, Alex took it dutifully and kissed his ring. The effect on her was immediate.

"Alex?" Lily's worried voice filled the room and Death set his eyes on her.

"So, this is the human I tasted before. Delicious again to be sure. I understand from Rowena here that you owe me your life."

"Lily doesn't owe you anything." Alex said forcefully. She tried to shake off the effect of kissing the ring and stood tall beside Lily. "I do."

"You?" He looked back at Rowena before facing Alex. "I was given to understand-"

"Rowena is lying."

"Reaper whore!" She screamed. "Sir, I told you the truth. This human was destined to die twenty years ago. Alex stole her from you and now she's here to do it again."

Alex fought to keep her temper under control.

Death walked past them all and took a seat, "Alexandra, is this true?"

Alex shook her head. "Not exactly."

Death rapped the armrest with his knuckles. "Enough of this! This creature is to be hunted soon and yet here she is. Why have you brought her before me if not to claim her and fulfill her destiny."

Alex put Lily behind her and stepped up to him. "I am here to demand her life."

If Death was surprised at her request, he didn't show it.

"Demand...you have the right if none other claim her."

"I claim her!" Rowena pushed past them both. "She was stolen from me twenty years ago. I claim the right to take her life now."

"Well..." Death considered the Reapers in front of him. They were the best he had and they were fewer and fewer. Losing either one would be difficult, but the choice was clear. "It looks to me like we have the makings of an old-fashioned duel."

The response to his words was immediate. Alex cursed, Rowena laughed and Lily was dumbstruck. Who the hell dueled anymore?

"A duel." Alex said. Her flat tone was pensive and Lily tried to figure out what was going through her head.

"Alex, you can't. Not for me. Let them take me, please."

"Are you that eager to die?" Death was curious about this human. She hadn't cowed before him which was impressive all by itself.

"No, I'm not, but I have always believed myself to be in control of my own destiny."

"Now you know the truth."

"I refuse to admit that I don't have a say. And I refuse to let anyone fight over me." She glared at Alex, angry for putting herself in this position.

"You would do it for me Lily." There was emotion in her voice unlike other Reapers.

Lily could only stare, Alex was right, she would fight for her.

"Interesting." Death spoke more to himself than them. "We are agreed then. I cannot let what happened go without some payment. A life is a life after all. And your pictures will stop, one way or another this way. We can't have everyone knowing when Death comes for them."

"When?" Rowena growled. It was easy to tell she wanted to go right then.

"Tomorrow, my arena. At the moonrise. I will provide the weapons of course." He brushed an imaginary speck of dust from his pants before standing up.

"You are to stay away from each other until the arena. If I hear different, we will have a different sort of problem."

Alex nodded and grabbed Lily by the hand. "Yes sir." She stared at Rowena one last time before shimmering away with Lily.

"This is crazy." Lily watched as Alex dug through her duffel. "Alex, don't ignore me."

"I'm not ignoring you." She kept rifling until she found what she was looking for. The plain envelope she pulled out was nondescript, but it was sealed and addressed to Lily.

"I need you to have this in case anything happens." Alex seemed embarrassed to hand over the letter.

"I don't understand?" Lily turned the letter over in her hands. "What is this?"

"It's a letter I wrote you...after you left."

When Lily started to open it, Alex snatched it away.

"Please...only if this doesn't go well."

Lily opened her mouth to say something and snapped it shut. It wasn't like Alex to hesitate when she spoke. She was always so sure of herself.

"This is really happening, isn't it?"

"It is." Alex pulled her into her arms. "I told you, I *will* fight for you."

"Yes but-"

"No buts. I love you Lily. I didn't know it for what it was, but I know it now and all I want is for you to survive. I need you to survive."

When Alex kissed her, Lily let herself forget about the letter and what was to come.

HER KISSES WERE gentle and inviting, with a tenderness that wasn't there before.

Tears rolled down her cheeks as Lily realized that in her own way, Alex was telling her goodbye.

"Hey," Alex's husky voice filled her heart. "Why are you crying?"

Lily grabbed her by the back of the head and kissed her forcefully.

"This is not goodbye, dammit!"

Alex wiped away her tears and smiled.

"Never goodbye Lily. Never goodbye."

CHAPTER
TWENTY-SEVEN

When they showed up at the arena, Lily was immediately separated from Alex.

"What the hell Basque?" The tone in her voice was frightening.

"Sorry Alex. Death's orders. He wants to make sure the debt is paid regardless of the outcome." He did sound sorry, even as he bound Lily's hands.

Lily had been in control of her own life since the death of her parents. Now, her life was in the hands of beings she never even knew existed.

Two Reapers on opposite sides of her life. One wanted her dead and the other was willing to give up her own life to keep her alive.

The arena was deceptively large. She watched as the seating area filled with creatures she had only ever heard of in stories and folklore. But they were real. All of this was real.

Death stepped out onto the main floor and raised his hands. The immediate hush was unnerving.

"Welcome everyone, welcome. By now I'm sure you are all

aware why we are here. Twenty years ago, I was cheated of a life thanks to one of my best Reapers. Today we are here to rectify that. Rowena has challenged Alexandra for the life of this human." He pointed to Lily an ugly grin on his face. "No matter the outcome tonight, Death will be satisfied and all claim to this human, forfeit to the victor."

He waved over his guard. Two of them entered the arena with a mahogany chest and placed it in the center of the arena floor.

"The combatants will choose their weapons."

That's when she saw them. Alex and Rowena entered from opposite ends of the arena coming together at the chest. The guard opened the chest and both Reapers reached for the same style weapon.

They resembled a scythe only instead of being as tall as each of them, as Reapers were generally portrayed having, they were small enough to be held in each hand. That was where the similarity ended. At the end of each handle was a three-inch blade, making it deadly at both ends.

According to Basque who seemed quite content to explain things to her, the weapons were known by many names, but most called them Kamas. They seemed to hum with an unknown energy.

Both Reapers were dressed all in black. Alex wore the same clothes she'd worn on the day she reconnected with Lily.

She threw Lily a wan smile as both Reapers walked over to their respective edge of the arena.

***

Alex was allowed to speak to Lily one last time before they started.

"Hey."

Lily pushed Basque away and leaned into Alex, relishing the feel of her arms around her.

"Why those?" Lily eyed the weapons in Alex's hands and shuddered at the potential damage they could do. Beside the curved blade at one end of the weapon, the evil looking blade that protruded from the handle allowed for damage to be inflicted no matter which side of the weapon connected.

But they were Reapers, immortal.

Alex hefted the weapons in each hand.

"The blades are imbued with the same properties as his ring." Alex tried to sound confident.

"You mean...you can...die?" Lily didn't bother pretending she wasn't terrified. Both could hear the tremor in her voice.

Alex leaned down and captured her lips, eliciting a groan from Lily and a slew of hateful epithets from Rowena.

"It doesn't matter Lily. Either way, you'll be free."

Lily felt her heart start to break as the Reaper walked out into the arena with a whispered "I love you."

Neither made mention of the weapon's resemblance to the scar on Lily's chest.

THE HUSH that fell over the crowd was immediate as both Reapers stepped into the arena.

They met in the center where the chest, now removed, had been placed.

"We don't need to do this Rowena. We can say no."

"We can't, and I won't. You turned your back on me twenty years ago for that." She threw a glare Lily's way. "You betrayed us. You betrayed Death and now he knows it. You've gotten away with being his pet for too long."

"You're a fool Rowena. I've never been his pet. We're

Reapers, pure and simple. We do what we do because it is our lot in life. I just happened to be the first one to choose to say no."

"You aren't the first, but you will be the last." With that confusing statement, Rowena lunged at her barely missing her face.

"Dammit!" Alex dove to one side and rolled over her shoulder, coming back to a crouching position. Rowena was fast and deadly, but then so was she.

She launched herself at the other Reaper, weapons clashing.

Neither of them was able to cut the other, not for lack of trying, until Rowena threw an elbow that caught Alex across the temple and knocked her flat.

"ALEX!"

Lily's warning added to the roar of the crowd as Alex got up on all fours shaking her head. The blade headed her way slashed her across the back.

Alex's scream was chilling.

Scrambling away she got up and faced Rowena.

A hush came over the crowd as they squared off again.

ALEX KEPT an eye on Rowena's blades. Like her own, they were imbued with the same magic as Death's ring. That one slice had already started to sap her energy.

She looked over at Lily, bound now at Death's side and knew she had to win this battle for her.

Rowena caught her glance and cried. "Even now? Even now

you can't stop looking at her. Are you so willing to end your existence for her? For a human?"

She flinched at the raw pain in Rowena's words. She could feel the Reaper's rage and perceived betrayal.

Alex didn't know what she ever saw in her apprentice and she regretted every moment that she had given of her time and to what she thought had been love.

Love...she hadn't known love until Lily.

Her heart throbbed with the love she had for her. She thought back to what the old man had said about his wife when she had collected his soul. What Selena and even Death himself had said and the answer was a resounding yes.

"Yes Rowena, I am."

The other Reaper's roar of rage wasn't her only response and Alex barely managed to fend of Rowena's attack. Blades sparked in unison as they clashed.

The handheld scythes were easily handled and quite deadly, and thus, the weapon of choice for Reapers. Unfortunately, Alex hadn't practiced with them in over a hundred years and it was obvious Rowena had.

Moving to the left she felt one of the blades slice the side of her face as she swiped at Rowena's back. The tearing of the reaper's coat showed just how close Alex got to connecting, and Rowena knew it.

She followed up her attack with a back kick that caught Alex in the side, knocking her against the stone enclosure.

Alex rose to one knee and brushed the hair out of her face, preparing for Rowena's next onslaught.

"Temper, temper Rowena." Alex's taunting was all for show and got her the exact response she wanted as Rowena charged her again.

CHAPTER
TWENTY-EIGHT

Lily fought desperately against her bindings.

"Alex, stop! Let them take me!"

Her pleas fell on deaf ears as the two Reapers circled each other again, the cut along Alex's back and cheek had weakened her, just as the cuts now on Rowena's arms and torso had weakened her, but there was no stopping either Reaper.

Selena had warned her of the cost Alex would pay for loving her and she had refused to accept it. She glared at the Reaper standing guard over her.

"Please...Basque, right? Please let me go. Let me help her." Tears of frustration rolled down her face as she spoke.

Basque bit his lip and she pounced on his uncertainty.

"You know this is wrong." She cried. "How can you all allow this to happen?"

The clashing of blades drew her attention back to Alex.

Horrified she watched as Alex swerved away from the blade edge that sliced her way. Rowena's viciousness made itself apparent when she turned the weapon around and stabbed at Alex. The jab caught Alex in the stomach and her cry of pain echoed through the chamber resounding against the walls and the growing bloodlust among the Reapers and other beings gathered.

"Alex!" Helpless she watched Alex drop to her knees and glared at Death.

"Stop this dammit!"

Death ignored her, clapping his hands together.

"Come now Alexandra…your human will pay the price for your failure."

Alex blocked another strike from Rowena, locking their blades together. Both Reapers grunted with the effort of maintaining a grip on them. Alex was the first to make a move, placing a leg against Rowena's hip and pulling her toward her as she dropped to the ground.

The roar of approval from the crowd in response to the judo throw was as unexpected as the throw itself. Rowena landed flat on her back both weapons dropping from her hand.

"Alex, don't." Lily fought against the ties even as Basque surreptitiously loosened the binding on her hands.

Alex rolled onto her knees, weapons still firmly in hand. Her rasping breaths filling the room as she continued to bleed from her wounds. Dragging herself over to Rowena she mounted her and held a blade to her neck.

Shaking off the lightheadedness that threatened to overwhelm her, she held the weapon as steady as she could. Rowena seemed stunned by the sudden turn of events.

"Don't do it." Rowena's emotionless plea made her pause.

"I never said I would."

"Finish it." Death snapped his fingers at Basque and smiled broadly when he dragged Lily over to him. "Finish it or she dies Alexandra. That was the arrangement you made."

"Why? Why does anyone need to die?"

"What?" He looked affronted at her words. "You are a Reaper, Alexandra Dante. Nothing more, nothing less."

"Nothing more?" Alex caught herself as Rowena bucked underneath her. She looked down as Rowena struggled to reach one of the blades she had dropped.

"No! No more!" Enraged, Alex brought the pointed handles down and through Rowena's shoulders, pinning her to the floor as her screams pierced the chamber.

Alex ignored it and stood unsteadily. They were definitely on equal footing now, the blades sapping each of their strength.

She stood wavering before Death in defiance.

"Let Lily go!" She demanded.

Confused, she watched as his initial anger at her challenge morphed into satisfaction.

"Alex, lookout!" Finally, free of her bindings, Lily ran out just as a bloodied and battered Rowena rose to stab Alex in the back.

Lily's look of shock as the blade plunged into her chest silenced everyone, including Rowena.

"LILY!!"

Lily turned, impaled with Alex's own weapon, and fell into her lover's arms.

Chaos erupted as the rules of the duel were dismantled with that one act. Death dealt quickly with Rowena, her lifeless body a stark reminder of another soon to follow.

Alex's cries filled the chamber as Lily struggled for breath.

"Lily...no, please..." She hesitated before pulling out the

blade trying desperately to stave off the inevitable as Lily's blood flowed between her fingers. She put her hand over the wound that had pierced the scar on Lily's chest hoping their connection could save her.

"NO!!"

She felt nothing. No heat, no spark, she had nothing left.

The damnable blades had done their job and she could feel Lily's life-force flickering in her arms.

"Alex…" Lily whispered as she touched Alex's face. "Let me go…"

"No…" She didn't care that she was crying and turned to face Death. "Undo this. This wasn't supposed to happen. It was supposed to be me. I am still willing to give up my soul for her." She spared Rowena's lifeless form a glance. "You have your life! You don't need hers!"

She was screaming and she didn't care.

"This one is not up to me Alexandra."

Shock coursed through her. Regret, she heard regret in Death's voice, but that was impossible.

A whispered breath brought her back. "Alex…" Lily was as pale as she'd been on that night twenty years before.

"Lily. I'm sorry Lily I-" She choked back a sob.

"Shhh…" Lily caressed her cheek. "…love…you…" Eyes closed, her hand dropped to her side.

The silence in the chamber was deafening.

"No…" Alex refused to accept what had just happened and just as she had inadvertently done twenty years earlier, she did what only one Reaper before her had ever done.

Twenty years ago, at the edge of death, Lily had been pulled from the brink by the unexpected burst of emotion and remorse of a Reaper.

Alex had fulfilled a prophecy written long before, a

prophecy she knew nothing about. She knew now she was the harbinger of death, but she could also be the harbinger of life.

Energy spent she summoned the reserves of her will and placed her hands over the now open scar on Lily's chest, pouring her soul into the woman she loved. She breathed a sigh of relief as Lily drew a breath, even as she drew her last.

CHAPTER
TWENTY-NINE

A stunned silence filled the chamber as the spectators realized what had happened. The human at the center of the challenge was alive, while two Reapers lay dead.

Basque rushed out not even sparing a glance for his former boss. Kneeling next to Alex, he hesitated before rolling her over. The half-smile on her face made it seem like she was sleeping.

He allowed himself to look over at the woman who was at the root of all that had happened. The wound on her chest had sealed itself and angry raised ridges of a new scar were beginning to form.

Now what? He turned back to where Death was standing and was surprised to see Selena, the bartender from the Hotel talking to him.

Everyone was being removed from the chamber by Death's personal guard and they were not happy.

When Rowena was carried past him, he realized he felt nothing. Her hatred had been her downfall. He sat there between the lovers thinking about his conversation with Death.

Death had told him he would play a part in this reckoning, but he had never been told how. Now he knew. He was to be the archivist. This story's story teller. Reapers all over the world respected and feared Alexandra Dante as a Reaper and now...after this...

"She is not gone Basque." Death placed a hand on his shoulder, his voice grim. "But she will be if we don't act quickly."

Death picked Alex up himself. "Grab the girl and come with me." He stormed away heading into his great room, Selena following closely behind.

Lily could feel Alex lying with her and she felt her body relax, the tightness in her chest easing. The fight was a dream, it had to be. She felt as close to Alex now as she had when they'd first lain together, when Alex had run her fingers along her scar igniting a fire within them both. She felt like she was home.

She fought to open her eyes, but they were so heavy, the effort it took was incredible and she felt the strain in every fiber of her being. When she finally opened them, she found herself in a room she was not familiar with. It certainly wasn't Alex's hotel room.

Rolling over, she groaned at the pressure she felt in her chest and gasped as she remembered.

Her fingers felt along the fresh scar as tears gathered in her eyes. Where was Alex?

She was alone in the large room, but she could hear voices.

Holding on to the couch she stood and waited for the room to stop tilting around her. She must have made a noise because suddenly, she wasn't alone.

"You're awake." Basque shimmered in beside her and was rewarded with a slap to the face.

"What the hell lady?" He grabbed her hand and pushed her back roughly.

"Enough Basque." Death stood in the now open doorway looking more somber than she'd ever seen.

"Where is Alex? What have you done to her?"

Death ran a hand through his hair and cursed.

"*I* didn't do anything to her."

"Stop it Edward." Selena's admonishment shocked her into silence as did her use of his name.

"Selena."

"Do not use that tone with me. It didn't work for Alex and it won't work for you."

Lily lurched to her feet. "Stop it! What happened? Where is Alex?"

She saw them exchange a look, but no one said a word.

"Goddamn you! Where is she?"

Alex lay still as death in the great room where they'd come to plead for Lily's life.

"No…" Lily stumbled when she got to her, falling to her knees.

"Do something." She cried.

Selena and Death exchanged a glance.

"I can't. She must want to come back and I've done all I can. She is alive, but the rest is up to her."

He took Selena by the arm and headed to the door. "Talk to her Lily. She is tied to you, now more than ever."

Lily let them leave, turning her attention back to Alex. She had never seen her this still. It was unnerving.

She looked like she was sleeping. Her black shirt was torn in several places where Rowena's blades had sliced through, most notably in the front where she'd been stabbed. She reached in and touched what was now an angry scar and snatched her hand back. Alex's skin was neither warm nor cold.

"Alex dammit don't you dare do this to me." She placed a hand over her own scar and hugged herself as she slid to the floor. "I can't go through this again." Her harsh sobs echoed in the large room.

She cried. Alternating between holding Alex's hand and speaking to her about the future they could have, she cried.

She thought again about the manuscript and how it might apply. Maybe Alex finally was at peace. No! She couldn't give up on her. She wouldn't.

Anger and grief overwhelmed her and she grabbed a statue, smashing it against the floor. The exploding pieces mimicked the pieces of her heart. She was okay being alone before. Not anymore.

She didn't know if it was her anger or if she could hear Alex whisper to her but that was when she remembered the letter.

SHE FELT around in the pocket of her pants and pulled out the envelope which was now stained brown. Shocked, she looked down at the front of her jeans. They looked like they were covered in rust stains, and her shirt too was stained with what she knew was her blood and torn where she'd been stabbed.

That was when it hit her, what no one had bothered to explain.

"This is my fault." She was alive because Alex had again done whatever she had done twenty years ago, only this time...

"This time, she didn't have enough to share."

Death strode into the room and went immediately to check on Alex.

"How did you know what I was thinking?" She demanded.

"Humph...It's a simple thing really, for me."

"Alex does it...did it?" Her confusion was palpable.

"Does she now?" His chuckle was like a small rumble. "That's my girl."

"Your girl? You got her killed!"

"No, I gave her a chance. I gave you both a chance. That is not what I'm normally known for you know."

Lily fought the urge to hit him. The flippant way he was speaking about Alex, about them, hurt her to her very soul.

"Aargh...You are infuriating! What the hell did you mean 'she didn't have enough to share.' Share what?"

"Her life force." When he saw the confused look on her face, he changed tactics. "Sit down little girl."

She would've argued with him, but his voice was compelling.

"Twenty years ago, Alexandra shared something, with you, a human, that she wasn't meant to. When she did that, she opened up a connection that hasn't existed since her conception."

Lily clutched the unread letter in her hands and tried to process what he was telling her.

"Her conception...oh my God...it was you." Lily scrambled to her feet. "It was your journal. You're the harbinger. You're her father?"

Her disbelief would have been funny in any other circumstance. She looked from him to Alex and wondered why she hadn't seen it before, why no one had.

"No one was ever meant to know little girl. Not even Alexandra." He seemed uncomfortable with the admission.

"Then why? Why would you allow her to fall in love and put her through all of this?"

"She was born to fulfill a prophecy. She was born to die. For love."

CHAPTER
THIRTY

Lily watched with a wary eye as Basque came in with a tray of food.

"He wants you to eat."

"He needs to go to hell." He flinched at the bitterness in Lily's voice and backed out without another word.

Death had finally left her in peace after spending another ten minutes trying to explain. Alex was not dead, but she wasn't alive either according to him. She didn't care about the rest of what he had to say. All that mattered was Alex and she heard enough to understand that she was the key to bringing Alex back.

"Alexandra Dante, I'm about to read this letter and so help me, it better have some answers because I don't know what to do." She dropped a tender kiss onto her lips and sat down to read.

Dear Lily,

If you are reading this, then you came back. It hurts me to write this part, but if you are reading this then something has also happened to separate us.

Over a year ago you almost met Death face to face, again. Seeing you lying there, broken on those rocks, forced me to reveal myself to you. I am smiling as I write this because I know you do not remember, you weren't exactly yourself and I was unable to stay with you while help came, but I was with you. I've been with you your whole life. You told your aunt once that you believed you had a Guardian Angel. That was almost true. You had a Guardian Reaper.

Yours is the first life I have ever wanted to preserve with every ounce of my being. There is a beauty to your soul unlike that of any other, a grace that humanity takes for granted. I vowed to watch over and protect you, and I have. If you are reading this though, your life has taken an even stranger turn. You are now aware there is more to the world than the things you see every day.

I hoped to be the one to help you navigate this new awareness but as I said, if you are reading this, something has happened. Please know it will have been worth it, if you are alive.

I hope by now I've told you I loved you, and I do. I have been alive for longer than I would like to admit and while I have seen love, I've never understood it. Until now.

When you were attacked in your apartment I almost violated Death's edict and took a life that wasn't mine to take. It scared me. I've never lost control before but my feelings for you were and are...overwhelming.

I'm rambling I know...I know where this will end. Death wants a life and thanks to Rowena and my actions twenty years ago yours is forfeit. I refuse to accept that. If given the chance I will challenge Rowena for your life.

My love, if you are reading this, I lost. But you are alive and that means I will live in your heart as you have lived in mine. I truly wanted a future with you, I wanted...so much more than I deserve.

Just know that I am at peace knowing you are alive. The days we spent together were more than I could ever have hoped for and I can only hope that you felt something for me. Let Death have his life, I will die before he takes yours.

We are connected, even unto death. Don't forget that. Don't let my passing stop you from living. The moment I held your hand I felt whole. You did that. Our connection and our love did that. I refused to let you die twenty years ago and I refuse to let you now.

My soul aches as I write this, but you need to know that you have my love for all eternity. The love of a Reaper.

Yours ForeverAlexandra Dante

"Damn you Alex," she whispered. Of course she loved her. She had tried to stop Rowena but-

"I'm the key." Anguish tore at her. She placed a trembling hand over the scar on her chest. "Why Alex? Why couldn't you let me go?" She put her other hand on Alex's chest. "Come back to me Alex. He says you were born to die for love. I can't let you. You deserve better, you deserve more." Her heart wrenching sobs echoed in the great room.

"Dammit Edward, help her." Selena couldn't keep the anger out of her voice.

"Selena, I cannot. If the girl can't bring her back, then my daughter is lost to us." Edward felt an unfamiliar pang of remorse. He had waited so long for Alexandra to fulfill her destiny, that he had created an unnecessary barrier between himself and Alexandra.

Her mother had been human and she'd died during childbirth. Alex had been raised in this very house, but she didn't remember her youth thanks to Selena. Hell, she considered the Hotel her home, not here. She had always known she was a Reaper though and she was a damn good one. He was proud of her, but he was truly helpless here.

The connection between Lily and Alexandra was strong enough to overcome Death.

It was stronger even than the connection he'd had with her mother.

Lily was capable of bringing her back, she just needed to figure it out on her own.

***

LILY FELT her hand tingle and snatched it back. *Not possible.* She shook out her hand and looked at her fingers, they were still tingling.

"Oh my God…" She put her hand back on Alex's chest and clenched her teeth when she felt a strong jolt up her arm. "Fight Alex…please. You said you loved me, don't leave me. Please…don't leave me damn it!"

CHAPTER
THIRTY-ONE

Lily...She could hear her, feel her, but that was impossible. Pain and fire raged through her, exploding in her chest. She could hear Lily more clearly now, still distant, but clearer. *Lily*...

The darkness had been welcoming at first, but a devastating loneliness had taken hold of her here. Her last memory, of Lily dying in her arms, was overwhelming and all she wanted was to let go. Was it real? Had she managed to save her? She clung to the love she felt for her. If she was here, then maybe she had managed to save Lily after all.

"Alex!"

Pain raged through her again and she could hear her clearly.

"I love you Alex Dante, don't you dare die on me!"

"Don't...yell." Her voice was barely a whisper, but she may as well have yelled it when a sobbing Lily fell on top of her, showering her with kisses.

Lily was exhausted and her hand was throbbing from the charge it had released into Alex. Two times. It had taken two times to bring her back and she felt what it had cost her, but she didn't care.

"You're back!" She planted a kiss on her lips that the Reaper immediately returned.

Alex let out a groan when she tried to move, and Lily immediately pulled back.

"No...help me up." Alex grabbed Lily's arm and felt the welcoming hum of their connection.

Lily was speechless when she felt it too.

"Is this our new normal?" She asked.

Alex shrugged, disoriented.

Lily could tell she was still in a lot of pain.

"It is." Death said.

When he walked in Alex immediately stood up and placed herself between him and Lily.

"Stay away from her." Alex's guttural tone made him take a step back.

"Alexandra..." The warning in his voice was unmistakable.

"No-" She grabbed Lily in a viselike grip and shimmered away.

She collapsed as soon as they reappeared in Lily's living room.

"Alex!"

Lily caught her before she hit the floor, grateful for all her years of climbing. The lanky Reaper was heavier than she looked and she half dragged, half carried her to her bed.

Fear took over for just a moment until she saw Alex's chest rise and fall.

"Dammit Alex." Exhausted, she sat on the floor next to the bed to catch her breath. It seemed like ages since she'd been in her own home. The Hotel was nice and had become quite comfortable, since she associated it with Alex, but this was her home. *They* were home.

When she finally climbed onto her bed, she held onto Alex, letting exhaustion and relief whisk her away.

WHEN ALEX OPENED HER EYES, she felt almost like herself again. The feel of Lily's body lying next to hers was pure bliss and she allowed herself to revel in it before she finally got up.

Lily didn't move when she got up giving Alex a chance to fall in love all over again. She brushed away a strand of hair from Lily's face and smiled at her response.

She could feel the call of Death, stronger now than ever. Work was work, but this, being here with Lily, this was life. Life she now knew was possible.

"Hey..." Lily's sleepy voice interrupted her. "Is everything okay? Are you?" She started to sit up.

"Sleep...I'll be here when you wake up."

Alex watched as her voice lulled Lily back to sleep.

Knowing she was alive and here with her made her feel connected finally. To life and love.

When she felt the call again, she knew there was no ignoring it and as much as she wanted to stay, she left.

LILY WRINKLED her nose as the smell of bacon finally dragged her from her sleep but then she smelled something else, herself. She was rank, still covered in her own blood and her clothes...

"Ugh." She allowed herself a little smile though. She was alive. They were both alive and knowing what led to the wretched event in the arena made her wonder what else was in store for them. She crawled out of bed and walked straight into the bathroom. She wanted to see Alex but for once in her life, vanity won out.

Alex heard the shower and got started on eggs. She had spent the better part of the day responding to calls and making herself presentable.

The looks on the faces of hotel patrons when she had walked through the lobby had been priceless and something she would cherish forever. She had forgone going to the bar knowing that Selena was sure to be present when she finally confronted Death.

Lost in her thoughts, she hadn't heard the water stop and when she turned around, Lily launched herself at her. This was a different Lily. There was no melancholy, there was just a brightness, a light to her soul that hadn't been there since her parents' death.

"Wow. We should do this more often." She practically growled as the half-naked woman in her arms kissed her.

"Die? No...I don't think so." She held her at arm's length. "Are you really okay?"

Alex took one of her hands and placed it over her heart. "I am"

Lily plopped down on a chair. "So, what now?"

"Now, we eat. Then we play, because later we have an appointment with Death."

CHAPTER
THIRTY-TWO

"You're nervous." The forced humor in Alex's voice was not at all funny to Lily.

"Aren't you? The last time we were here..." She looked around the room where Alex had basically been lying in state waiting...for what? Waiting for her according to Death, or Edward as Selena called him. She hadn't said very much to Alex about what had transpired, and she didn't think it mattered.

There was an air of confidence and swagger around Alex that was decidedly more pronounced than it had ever been. She just hoped it was still there when she found out the truth about who she was.

"Hey...where did *you* go this time?" Alex threw her own words back at her.

Lily didn't get a chance to answer before the doors opened.

Alex stiffened when Basque came in first followed by Death and then Selena. She looked over at Lily and wondered what was going on in her head. She couldn't read her right now and that was as disconcerting as the individuals who had walked in.

"Alexandra...Lily...you both look well." Death's magnanimous tone grated on her, but she was determined to hear him out.

"No thanks to you."

"Ah, but Alexandra it is all thanks to me." He spared Lily a glance.

"Did she not tell you?"

"Tell me what?" She said warningly.

"First let me just say that I am happy you are feeling like yourself again. And you are, aren't you?"

"I am," she said carefully.

"Oh, relax Alexandra. I'm not trying to trick you. I'm trying to explain."

"Enough games Edward." Selena broke her silence and looked at Alex.

"You are the product of the union in the manuscript. And this fool-"

"Watch your tone!"

Selena ignored him. "Is your father."

"You are more than just a Reaper, Alexandra."

Alex looked at Lily in disbelief. "You knew?"

"He told me when we thought...when I thought..."

Alex squeezed her hand tightly. She couldn't be angry with her, none of this was her fault.

"Did I die?" When he tried to explain, she stopped him.

"Just answer the damned question. Did I die?"

"Yes and no. You are tied to me as my daughter, but she was the only one who could bring you back. You are forever connected, even unto death."

"What-" She swallowed the unfamiliar emotion she was feeling. "What happened to my mother? Was she human?"

"She was," he said sadly. "She died in childbirth. There had been no Reaper/Human births before you. And considering who you fell in love with...there likely won't again." He didn't sound bitter as much as sad.

"I'm your daughter...I'm your daughter and you put me, us, through hell?" Anger flared and her tone changed, making Basque take a step back.

"I helped you fulfill your destiny!"

"What destiny? To die? To fall in love? Which one?" Even Lily took a step back as she railed against him.

"To survive. You are destined to fill my role in the future and the only way you could was to experience life. That meant love and death."

"I hate you." She ground out.

"Maybe, but not forever." He tried to sound confident, but they all heard the hint of uncertainty in his voice.

LILY LOOKED out over the lobby of the Hotel from the third-floor landing. It really was beautiful here. She thought about their treatment upon their arrival a few hours ago, after their meeting with Death. They had created quite a stir.

Ava at the front desk had squealed and come around the counter to hug them both. Some Reapers had approached Alex with congratulations and others to beg for forgiveness. Apparently, it was a small enough world at the hotel that everyone was now aware of who Alex truly was.

Lily hugged herself tight. Alex had been so upset when they had gone back to her place that she had proposed going to the Hotel. Once there, Alex had followed a familiar pattern for a different reason and left her to go discuss a few things with Selena and a friend from her old school. This time though, Lily knew she was free to roam, and roam she did until she found this view.

Here in this spot she could almost tell how big the Hotel was. A view like this just a few days ago would have overwhelmed her, but now, her life had taken such a strange turn, she wondered if she could ever go back and live her life as she had. The drive to tempt fate and death was gone.

"Beautiful, isn't it?" The sound of Alex's boots echoed against the far wall as she came up behind her.

"Mmmm…" She leaned back into Alex's arms relishing the feel of her arms around her.

"You know…this is one of the few places I've ever called home. Her husky voice held a hint of regret.

"I know." She wondered where this was leading. They hadn't discussed where they went from here as a couple, especially with the knowledge of her heritage.

"Would you consider…I mean will you…"

Now she understood.

"I don't know if I can stay here Alex, but you can come home with me." Her hopeful tone put a smile on Alex's face, and she nodded.

"Lily, I'll be honest, I don't know if that will work, hell I don't know what will, but I'm willing to try. Wherever you are will be home to me no matter where it is. Who knows," she said with a broad smile, "maybe we can use the Hotel as a vacation home?"

Lily nodded. That was certainly doable.

"By the way," Alex said, "Selena gave me this. Rowena had it in her pocket." She gave Lily the sketch she'd made of the Reaper.

She clutched the sketch to her chest before turning around and wrapping her arms around her.

She knew the shift in Alex's life matched her own, but they would face life together. She gently traced the scar on Alex's face, a visible reminder of all they'd been through, before she kissed her.

"I love you Alexandra Dante and I want to face life by your side."

"And Death, Lily, we will face life and death together."

CHAPTER 33
WHISPER OF DEATH
A FORBIDDEN REAPER ROMANCE

What happens when one assumes the Mantel of Death? With the realization of her heritage, Alex is forced to take on a more active role in the world of Reapers and paranormal beings.

As Alex struggles to navigate the Reaper hierarchy and the families within, she takes the step to plan a bonding ceremony with Lily.

Outside forces threaten not only her existence, but their love as well.

Betrayal comes from within in a Whisper of Death.

Coming Winter 2022

Check out Alex Dante in The Reaper Trials series
Reaper Trials Series

Acknowledgments

Special thanks to Danelle Sierra for helping me act out the main fight scene for this work, weapons and all.

Reapers have always fascinated me, and I am grateful to have been asked to write a story for The Hotel Paranormal Series that spawned my take on Reapers and this Reaper's Tale.

About the Author

L.E. Perez writes kickass women and paranormal creatures. Her tagline for all her works is Strong Women, Strong Stories.

Check in with her here and sign up for her newsletter for freebies, goodies and updates:

LE Perez Author

Made in the USA
Columbia, SC
06 June 2024